THE MAD SCIENTISTS OF NEW JERSEY

CHRIS SORENSEN

Happy Reading Alyssa!

HARMFUL MONKEY PRESS

Harmful Monkey Press / Sparta, NJ

Cover art by Doreen Mulryan
www.doreenmulryan.com

Chris Sorensen – First Edition

ISBN 978-0-9983424-0-5

Printed in the United States of America

FOR MOM & DAD

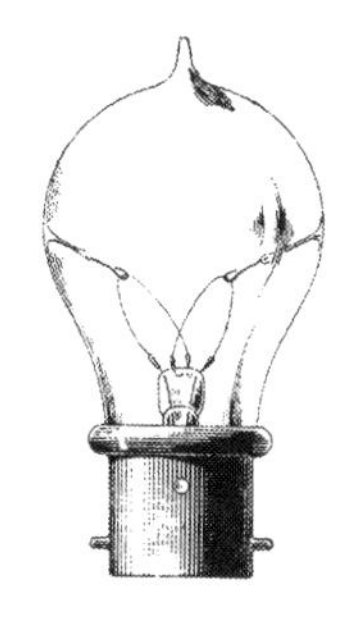

Prologue

Although he was already going fifteen miles over the speed limit, Bill Edison pressed his foot on the gas as lightning cracked overhead. The old clunker complained but gave him a bit more speed. Rain pelted the windshield, the only working wiper doing its best to give him a view of the road ahead.

Lake Mohawk lay to his right, its choppy surface alive with whitecaps. *Oh, if those dark waters could speak.*

A delivery truck blared its horn, and Bill swerved as it barreled past. Come on! Keep your eyes on the road!

He thought about Linda asleep at home. He thought about Eddie. Sport, he called him. He'd be in bed as well, curled up with their dog Cooper. His family. He had to keep them safe, no matter the result of tonight's meeting.

A shrill electric shriek echoed from the trunk, and the car lurched. What was that thing in the bag? And what powers did it possess?

Ever since it had come into his hands, Bill felt an unease he hadn't experienced since he was a child listening to the stories Abel told him when his parents weren't around. Stories about the old Edisons. Stories about the lake.

The Turtle Cove Diner appeared up ahead. The halogen lights, swaying in the wind, illuminated an empty parking lot. But not quite empty. An outdated station wagon sat parked around the corner near the employees' entrance.

Bill pulled up and turned off the engine. This was it. No turning back now.

He got out of his car and popped the trunk. Waves of rain assaulted him as he gathered up the thing in the canvas bag and headed for the diner.

Martha Sparks sat across from her husband Abel in a booth. She glanced up as Bill entered. She looked tired, Bill thought. He shook the rain from his jacket and walked over.

Abel was older than Martha. He sat bundled up in a flannel coat and scarf. He stared down at his plate of food, bewildered.

"Meatloaf? Who ordered meatloaf?" he snapped.

"You did, dear," said Martha. His wife for more than forty years, she said this with no malice, no impatience, as if his confusion were routine.

"Nonsense," said Abel. He started rummaging through his pockets and placed their contents on the table. Crumpled receipts, sticks of gum, a stray key.

Bill leaned in and kissed Martha on the cheek.

"Thanks for bringing him," he said.

"Always a treat getting him out of the house." Martha gave him a sad smile, letting him know that it was anything but.

Abel pulled more items from his pockets. A chewed-up stub of a pencil, paperclips.

The diner's lone waitress walked up with a coffee pot.

"Get you a menu?"

"No thanks," said Bill as he slid in next to Martha. The waitress yawned and headed back to the kitchen.

"Is that it?" Martha asked, pointing at the sack in his lap.

"It is," said Bill. He placed the sack on the table. Martha reached for it and hesitated.

"Where did you find it?"

"At a garage sale in Upper Lake. It was in a pail under a bunch of fishing gear. I guess one of the old families must have lived there at one point. Quite a bargain at seventy-five cents." Bill managed a smile.

Martha ran her fingers over the fabric. Was that warmth coming from within? Maybe it was just her imagination.

"Ah ha!" chortled Abel as he pulled an ancient electric razor from his pocket.

"Not now, Abel," moaned Martha. "You shaved this morning, remember?"

"Bah!" said Abel and he flicked on the razor and pointed it at his plate.

The razor hummed. Then it sparked. And then, the meatloaf on Abel's plate started to shimmer. Bill and Martha marveled as the meatloaf began to change shape before their eyes into...

"Pastrami on rye! Just like I ordered!" cried Abel. He was right. The meatloaf was gone, replaced by an overstuffed pastrami sandwich.

"Give me that thing before you turn us all into chickens," Martha said, grabbing the razor out of Abel's hand. Abel was too busy digging into his sandwich to mind the loss of his razor.

"May I?" asked Bill. Martha handed him the razor. Bill examined the seemingly innocuous item. "Runs on a destabilizing unit, I'd imagine. I wonder where he found it."

Martha sighed.

"You know our Abel. He's like a magpie. He picks up things here and there. On our morning walks around the lake, he's forever filling his pockets with this and that. Every now and then, he actually finds something useful. Something from the old days." She looked at her husband and reached over to tousle his hair. "Don't you, hon?"

"You're not getting one bite of this sandwich. It's mine."

"I know, hon," she said.

Thunder boomed in the heavens above the diner. The lights dimmed momentarily.

"I guess it's time you showed us," Martha said.

Bill slowly reached into the canvas sack and pulled out the device. It was roughly the size of a brick. And it was black. The entire surface of the thing was covered in interlocking gears.

Abel dropped his sandwich.

"What is it, Abel? Do you recognize it?" asked Bill.

The old man picked up the device, grasping it in his greasy hands. He turned it over and over, a look of fearful fascination on his face.

Finally, he set it back down on the table.

"Sly..." he whispered.

A chill tickled up Bill's back. Even though he had suspected as much, hearing the old man say the name caught him off guard. There wasn't much to know about the old days, about Sly. He had managed to cobble together only the briefest of histories, but one name came up again and again: Vernon Sly.

"This is one of his? You're certain of it? This is one of Sly's?" Bill asked.

As if in response, the overhead lights flickered again. Only this time, no lightning preceded it...

"What should we do with it?" Bill asked.

Martha stared down at the thing, her eyes narrowing to slits.

"Destroy it," she said.

"Destroy it now," Abel concurred.

The quiet was broken as a sound that was half train whistle, half roar erupted outside. Every light in the diner went out, plunging the place in darkness.

"Too late," Abel whispered.

Bill froze. What was that? It was a metallic sound, like a suit of armor stumbling just outside the window. *Clunk, clunk.* No, not armor – heavier than armor. Something mechanical. Something big.

Bill leaned in close to Martha.

"Whatever's out there is in the parking lot. Let's slip out the back, through the kitchen."

"You grab the device, I'll grab Abel," Martha said.

Bill reached for the thing on the table. It buzzed like an angry bee, and a flash of static electricity leapt up his hand. He dropped it onto the floor with a yelp.

A dim light began to seep from the device. Low at first, then streaming out from its innards through the clockwork of gears. A whirring sound rose from the thing as it sparked to life.

A pair of blazing red lights ignited outside the window, painting the diner red. The whistle shrieked again. Crash! A window shattered. Bill could hear the thing forcing its way into the diner.

"Get down!" Bill whispered. He pulled Martha to the floor, and the two of them worked to get Abel down with them.

"I can't find my sandwich!" Abel bellowed.

"Shh!" hissed Martha.

The gears on the device were spinning rapidly now, the whole metal surface alive with moving parts. Angry sparks leapt from within.

The door to the kitchen opened. A figure was silhouetted in emergency light. It was the waitress.

"Everyone okay in here?" she called as she stepped from the kitchen, a flashlight in her hand.

"Go back!" Bill yelled, but it was too late.

The red eyes turned toward the waitress. Her mouth fell open. The bulb in her flashlight exploded and then... she disappeared. The broken flashlight clattered to the floor.

Bill reached over and pulled the scarf from around Abel's neck.

"Hey!" squealed Abel.

Ignoring the old man's protests, Bill wrapped his hands in the scarf and reached out for the device. He could still feel the threat of electricity snapping from within, but he managed to get a good enough grip on it to raise it above his head and bring it down hard onto the linoleum floor.

The last thing Bill heard was the deafening sound of the horrible whistle. And the last thing he thought of was Eddie.

“Be strong, Sport,” he said. Then everything went red.

CHAPTER ONE

"Eddie Edison! Wake up!"

Eddie's eyes flew open as he jerked to attention, tossing his pen into the air in the process. It landed on the floor with a plunk.

"I... uh... what?" he stammered.

Mr. Hubbard retrieved the pen and slapped it on Eddie's desk. He leaned in, the smell of liverwurst sandwich on his breath.

"You will not sleep in my classroom, do you hear?" his teacher growled.

Eddie nodded quickly. He hadn't meant to doze off, but the way Mr. Hubbard droned on and on about fractions and decimals and... and...

"I said wake up!"

Eddie snapped up straight. Darn it! He'd fallen asleep again. And this time with Mr. Hubbard standing right over him.

"Sorry! Sorry!" Eddie cried. He glanced quickly to his left. Pudge was staring at his desk shaking his head. He was either laughing or trembling in sympathetic fear.

Mr. Hubbard sniffed. "Sleep on your own time, not on mine," he barked.

'Barked' wasn't that far off. Mr. Hubbard had the look of an old shelter mutt that no one would ever adopt. Stubble from his grizzled face sprinkled down the front his polyester shirt. His saggy dog eyes glared at Eddie from behind thick glasses.

Pudge snorted and quickly regretted it. Mr. Hubbard whirled on him. "Do you have something to add, Mr. Rizzotti?" Pudge shook his head, his double chin quivering.

"Good. Let's get back to this quadratic equation. Quadratic equations will be highly featured on this week's exam, so pay attention." Mr. Hubbard turned back to the chalkboard and began solving the problem with squeaking chalk, causing the entire front row of fifth graders to wince.

A piece of paper landed on Eddie's desk. He looked to Pudge who was pretending to examine the ceiling tiles. Smooth, Pudge. Real smooth.

Eddie unfolded the paper...

CHECK OUT THE NEW GIRL YET? WHAT'S UP WITH HER HAIR?

Eddie looked around the room. He hadn't noticed any new girl, and Mr. Hubbard had never taken time to announce new students. He always forced them to fend for themselves.

And then he saw her. Or rather, he saw her hair.

A great explosion of shocking red hair sat atop the body of the tall, skinny girl. Its effect was something like a fireworks display. Unlike the other girls in class who had just discovered primping and preening, this girl obviously couldn't care less about her tangled mass.

Eddie liked her immediately.

As if she could read his mind, the girl turned and looked back at him. Eddie gulped.

Her face was peppered with freckles, their rosy color setting off the ragged green sweater she wore. A sweater? In June? She curled her lip at him, an expression he couldn't quite interpret. Then she quickly turned away.

"And by taking the square root of both sides and isolating x, we come to our solution."

Mr. Hubbard picked up the eraser and stepped back. He turned to his dull-eyed class.

"Any questions before we move on?" No one moved. Finally, Jimmy Ticks, a nervous twerp, raised his hand. "Mr. Ticks?"

Jimmy looked at his own raised hand and went pale. Eddie could tell that, in his never-ending desire to please, Jimmy had raised his hand as a reflex, not because he had any question to ask.

"Yes, Mr. Ticks?" Mr. Hubbard tapped the eraser into his palm, puffs of chalk rising.

"Uhhh... what was... I mean, how did..." Jimmy stammered.

"Speak up, speak up!"

"Uhhh... what is x again?"

The eraser flew across the room so fast that Eddie was only aware that Mr. Hubbard had thrown it when Jimmy let out a startled cry. A rectangle of chalk dust decorated his dark blue shirt.

Tears welled up in Jimmy's eyes. Eddie saw red.

"Why don't you pick on someone your own size," Eddie blurted.

The entire class went silent, and Eddie knew he was in for it.

"What did you say?" Mr. Hubbard coughed.

"I said..." Eddie didn't know how to answer. He looked to Pudge. His friend was hiding behind his textbook.

Mr. Hubbard stepped closer. "Yes?"

"I said... why don't you put x over one on the side?"

His teacher stared at him, unsure of how to proceed. Eddie's response had obviously thrown him.

Not to be outmaneuvered, Mr. Hubbard grinned and held out a piece of chalk.

"Show us what you mean."

Eddie's mouth went dry. "To the board," Mr. Hubbard insisted.

Reluctantly, Eddie rose and made the trip to the chalkboard amidst the snickers of his classmates.

Leave it to moldy old Hubbard to still use chalk. Most of the other teachers at Lakeview School had laptops, iPads, interactive projections screens, the works. Not Mr. Hubbard. He seemed to take a certain gruff pleasure in banning those items from his class.

"Well, Mr. Edison?" Mr. Hubbard stood leaning against his desk, picking at his long nails.

Eddie slowly looked up at the board. The scrawled numbers and letters floated before his face like so much gibberish. He was doomed.

Eddie stalled. He pressed the chalk against the board. Too hard. The chalk snapped in two.

"No? Nothing?" asked Mr. Hubbard. "Just as I thought."

"Excuse me, sir?"

Mr. Hubbard looked around the room. "Yes? Who said that?"

The girl with the red hair stood up. She was even taller than Eddie had imagined. In fact, she was taller than Mr. Hubbard himself.

"Yes, Miss... Miss..."

"Roxie Michaels. This is my first day."

Mr. Hubbard stalked to his desk and flipped through a stack of papers. "Yes, Roxanne Michael. I have you coming in tomorrow."

"It's Michaels with an S. And it's Roxie, never Roxanne. And I was always coming in today. Always." The girl flashed Mr. Hubbard a smile that caught him off guard. Was she making fun of him?

"Did you have a question, Ms. Michael?"

Roxie twitched and said, "No, more of an observation, Mr. Cupboard."

"That's Hubbard."

"Whatever. It seems to me that we've gone a long time without any sort of break."

"What?" Mr. Hubbard snorted.

"I bet half the class could use a trip to the bathroom," she said, her eyes landing on Jimmy who was squirming in his seat at the mere mention of the word bathroom. "At my other school..."

Mr. Hubbard's face went pink. This seemed to please Roxie to no end. Eddie was dumfounded. She was saving his bacon, deflecting Mr. Hubbard's wrath.

"You are no longer at your other school, Ms. Michael. And if you were, you would no doubt be frolicking about on the playground or having afternoon ice cream or watching cartoons until your eyes fell out of your head!"

Eddie had never seen Mr. Hubbard this worked up. He had maybe come close that time the custodian had accidently thrown away his sack lunch, but this... this was definitely a new high.

He was totally unaware of his hand working the chalk across the chalkboard.

"But you are in my class, in my school," said the teacher. "You will sit down, Ms. Michael..."

"Michaels."

"...you will sit and you will learn to learn in silence. If that doesn't suit you, you can go down the hall and have a nice chat with Mr. Wood!"

A collective shudder went through the class. Mr. Wood, they said, was an ex-Marine who had once scared a kid so bad his hair turned white. No one risked a trip to Mr. Wood's office.

Roxie and Mr. Hubbard stared each other down, but the silence was broken by the rapid tap-tap-scratch of the chalk in Eddie's hand.

Mr. Hubbard fumed. "Mr. Edison, will you cut out that racket?" Eddie froze. Racket? What racket?

It was Pudge's gasp that warned him he should turn around. Eddie spun and stared at the chalkboard.

"What have you done?" Mr. Hubbard asked.

What indeed. Sprawled across Mr. Hubbard's neatly executed quadratic equation was a wave of numbers, symbols, letters and indecipherable squiggles.

In the midst of this chalky chaos, one sub-equation had been circled. It read:

H+U-BRD(-IZ)=A-J3RK

Eddie slowly worked it out. "Hubbard. Is. A... Oh, no!"

One by one, his classmates burst into laughter. Even Jimmy Ticks was laughing, although he had no idea why.

Eddie braced for impact.

Instead of exploding, Mr. Hubbard simply stared at the board for a long time. A very long time.

Then he started laughing. It was a frightening sound, like a weed whacker hitting gravel. He continued laughing as he made his way to his desk, opened the front drawer and pulled out his grade book.

"You seem to find yourself very amusing, Mr. Edison," he said as he flipped through the book. "Why don't we take a peek at your grades and see how funny you really are."

He sat on the edge of his desk and raised the grade book as if he was about to tell the class a story. "Let me tell you a story." *He was!*

"It begins back in September of last year with your fifth grade entrance exams. What kind of marks did you get, I wonder?" Mr. Hubbard was grinning. Did he have the right to do that? To read his grades out loud?

"Don't," Eddie said, but the old teacher silenced him with a wave of his hand.

"Reading: C-. Comprehension: C. Math..." Mr. Hubbard clucked his tongue, obvious pleased with his findings. "Mathematics: Incomplete. Science: D+."

"Stop it," Eddie said under his breath.

"I don't think so," Mr. Hubbard said. "You want the freedom to humiliate me in front of the class? Fine! Go ahead. But you must allow me to do the same."

He read on. History, social studies, composition. D, D-, F in that order. Eddie's face flushed. "That's enough," he said under his breath.

"Yeah, cut it out!" said Pudge.

"Would you like me to read your grades next, Mr. Rizzotti?" Mr. Hubbard smiled.

"I don't care," said Pudge. He was angry. "Go ahead and read 'em. But leave Eddie alone."

Roxie slapped her desk. "What he said, Cupboard."

Mr. Hubbard threw Roxie a nasty glare, collected himself and turned back to Eddie.

"Just the kind of friends I'd expect you to have, Edison. The pizza man's son and..." He looked Roxie up and down. "This one."

Eddie had had enough. He dropped the chalk on the floor.

"Leave them out of it."

Mr. Hubbard showed teeth. "Or what? You'll run home to your daddy?"

All the air left the room as the students took a deep breath in. Mr. Hubbard moved toward Eddie in mock apology.

"Oh, I'm sorry. I forgot your father is no longer in the picture. Disappeared, didn't he? Don't worry - I'm sure the authorities will round him up soon enough."

Eddie marched up to Mr. Hubbard, his hands balled into fists. He stared up at the smirking teacher.

"Eddie, no!" Pudge cried.

Eddie paused. And in that pause he saw his father. His father camping with him, his father fishing with him, his father sitting at the side of his bed reading to him before turning off the light.

Had Eddie not paused, he would have let loose with a string of swear words that would have impressed even Pudge, but instead he said, "Why, Mr. Hubbard. Your nose hair is in dire need of a trim. Your finger must get lost up in there."

Mr. Hubbard scowled.

The bell rang. The result was instantaneous. The class, already wound up with the tension of the moment, exploded toward the door.

Mr. Hubbard quickly pulled himself together enough to shout after them, "Proposals for your final science project are due tomorrow morning. Projects are worth one third of your science grade. Fail your project, fail the section."

Eddie backed away from the trembling teacher and went to his desk to gather his books. Pudge was instantly at his side.

"Come on, Eddie. Let's get while the gettin's good."

Eddie nodded, and he and Pudge scurried out of the room, leaving Mr. Hubbard glaring after them, his fingers fiddling with the hairs protruding from his nose.

The two friends threw open the front doors and trundled down the steps. Smell you later, Lakeview.

"Where you guys going?" asked a small voice behind them. They turned to find Jimmy Ticks standing on the steps, an unsure smile on his face. "Mind if I tag along?"

Pudge sighed. *Trapped!* "Ugh, this guy," he whispered. "You know my mom made me have him over to the house one time when we were kids. Just 'cause we went to Sunday school together. He just sat around reading books – didn't say a peep."

Jimmy was coming closer. "I asked if you minded if I tag along with you guys."

Pudge turned to the boy. "In one word, yes. We do mind."

Jimmy gave a nervous laugh. "That's four words, actually. Four. Yes... we... do..."

"Later, Ticks."

The boy got the point. He scurried off in the opposite direction even though his house was only a few blocks from both Pudge's and Eddie's.

Pudge got the conversation back on track. "I thought Hubbard was going to eat you alive back there."

"Nah," said Eddie, although he had actually thought the very same thing.

"Why'd he get so worked up, anyway?" Pudge asked as he pulled some beef jerky from his backpack and took a big bite. "Other guys in class have acted up way worse than you. Remember when Tully brought that rotten duck egg to class? Or when that Fenster kid pretended to have diarrhea in the lunchroom and then actually did have diarrhea in the lunchroom?"

Eddie shook his head. "I guess some people just like being jerks," he said, and it was one of the few things he had stumbled upon in his short life that he knew to be absolutely true.

"Your solution didn't work, you know," said a voice behind them.

The two boys turned. Standing behind them (and looking down at them) was the new girl, Roxie.

"Excuse me?" asked Eddie.

Roxie leaned her head to the side. "Your solution? H+U-BRD(-IZ)=A-J3RK? Funny. Didn't solve the problem in the least, but funny."

"How do you know he didn't solve it?" asked Pudge. He was staring at her hair.

Roxie shifted her gaze to Pudge. "Because I was at a private school before coming here, and we were studying this stuff back in fourth grade. That's how."

She smacked her lips and considered Eddie a moment before asking, "Have you two figured out your science projects yet?"

Pudge's grin was wide. "I figured we'd come up with something out on the boat."

Roxie leaned in and grabbed Pudge by the scruff of his shirt. For a moment, Eddie though she was going to either slap Pudge or kiss him.

"You have a boat?" she asked, a note of awe in her voice.

"Yeah," said Pudge, extracting himself from her grip. "It's just my dad's old pontoon boat. Why?"

The girl with the crazy hair took a step back.

"How about this," she said. "You take me out on your boat, and I'll help both of you come up with a killer science project idea. Remember, I'm two years ahead of you knuckleheads. What do you say?"

Pudge looked to Eddie. Why not? "All aboard!" he said.

Chapter Two

The Cheesy Breezy slowly putted its way toward the waters skirting the small island, Pudge sitting proudly behind the wheel of the pontoon boat. The vessel had seen better days. The vinyl seats were cracked, the carpet on the floor was worn and the motor hiccupped and spewed black smoke.

The man hiding in the bushes watched as the pontoon boat neared the island. He'd have to act quickly if this was going to work.

He opened his sack. The thing inside rustled in response. He stepped to the water's edge and emptied the sack. Something dropped into the murky water and disappeared.

"You call this a boat?" Roxie asked as she pulled the neck of her sweater up over her mouth to avoid the fumes.

"Give her a break. She runs, doesn't she?" Pudge asked. It was hard to take him seriously with the captain's hat he had perched on his head.

Eddie stared out across the water. It really was a beautiful day on Lake Mohawk. The water wasn't too choppy, and it looked as if the storm clouds that had threatened to ruin their boat ride were starting to disperse. Yes, a perfect day – if you weren't in danger of failing Mr. Hubbard's class.

He could just see his house across the lake. It was the one with the sagging roof, the faded siding, the yard desperately needing to be mown. He guessed he'd better get to it soon, but loud noise was the bane of his mother's existence.

A small fishing boat motored by, catching his attention. A burly father sat in the back steering, his son in a bright orange life vest up front. A lonely feeling swept over Eddie like a wave, and he had to swallow hard to keep it from spilling out.

"Earth to Eddie!" Pudge called.

Eddie shook the feeling off. "I was trying to figure out what to do for my project," he lied.

"We've got plenty of time for that," Pudge said as he cut the motor. He clambered over the back railing and tossed the anchor into the water. The rope played out quickly as the anchor made its swift decent to the bottom.

"What's that?" Roxie asked as she pointed at a small island a stone's throw away from where they sat anchored. A crumbling turret poked up over the tops of the scraggly trees that hid rest of the two-story house. The island was scarcely larger than the house itself.

"That's Echo Island," said Pudge. "No one's lived there for hundreds and hundreds of years."

Roxie squinted at the island. "From the looks of that turret I'd say the house was built in the early nineteen hundreds. Nineteen-ten, nineteen-eleven."

"Well, okay, maybe not hundreds and hundreds," Pudge snorted. "But it's been empty since my dad was a kid. He and some friends went over there to take a look. Said there wasn't much to see. Just a broken-down old house filled with trash."

Roxie shaded her eyes. "I think I saw something move."

All three trained their eyes on the brush that surrounded the house. Eddie felt in his gut that yes, he had seen something too. Was there someone hiding in the brush? But the longer he looked, the more he doubted his eyes.

"It's nothing. Come on, let's get some lines in the water before we start with my science project," Pudge said.

"Oh, we're starting with your project, are we?" Roxie asked.

"Gotta start somewhere," Pudge said with a grin. He attached a gaudy lure to his fishing line, drew back his pole and let the lure fly.

Eddie sorted through the tackle box, choosing a spinner for bass. He raised his pole and flipped his lure into the water. Roxie spent an annoyingly long time rummaging through the box, finally coming up with a rubber worm.

She slowly lowered her line into the water, leaned back and put her feet up. Her shoes were mismatched, different colors. Eddie wondered if she was making some sort of fashion statement.

"My left foot is smaller than my right," Roxie said, as if reading Eddie's thoughts. "Two sizes smaller." Her mouth curled in a proud, defiant grin.

Embarrassed, Eddie looked away. He wanted to ask what that had to do with the different styles, but instead he said, "Why are you here?"

"You said I could come."

"No, I mean, why are you *here*? In Lake Mohawk?" Eddie asked.

Roxie considered the question, seeming to roll it around in her head before taking a deep breath and saying, "I burned down my last school."

Pudge, who had just opened a strawberry soda and was taking his first sip, did a massive spit take. "You... what...?" he spluttered.

Roxie went red in the face. "I didn't mean to. It was just..."

"An accident?" Eddie offered.

"No. More like a misunderstanding. My old principal, Ms. Stanley, and I didn't see eye to eye. You may not have noticed, but I'm not like most girls my age."

As she said this, she was pulling a string of yarn from her sleeve, expanding an already existing hole in the shoulder. Eddie and Pudge didn't say a word.

"She thought anything that came out of my mouth was weird and therefore not to be believed," said Roxie. "And so when I told her that I had accidentally set our school mascot's costume on fire – it was a tortoise, and I was trying to reattach the shell with a soldering iron I'd borrowed from the custodian – she didn't even listen to me."

"And so the school burned down?" Eddie gasped.

"Well, not the whole school," she said. "It was mainly just the costume. But the art room was filled with smoke. I guess that's something you should know about me. I exaggerate. A lot."

She tossed her hair back and looked at Eddie for his reaction. She was an odd bird, definitely, but he gave her a nod letting her know he approved.

"Hey, Edison! You got something!" Pudge squealed.

Eddie certainly did have something. His line went taut and his pole bent nearly in two. He dug in his heels, leaned back and tried to reel in the line, causing it to twang angrily.

"You hooked a whopper!" Pudge shouted.

"You're going to lose it," Roxie said.

"No he won't!" said Pudge. "Why would you say that? You wanna jinx him? Come on, Eddie. Bring it in!"

Gritting his teeth, Eddie gave one final fierce tug and something shiny burst out of the water and into the air. Eddie watched as his catch flew over his head, hit Roxie in the knees and landed on the deck with a thump. "Owww!" Roxie howled. "Seriously?"

The three stared down at the thing. Silver in color, it was roughly the size of a basketball. To Eddie's eye, it looked like a large metal walnut.

"Congratulations. You caught a piece of junk," snorted Pudge.

Eddie's first impression of the thing proved to be very astute. The surface of the object had grooves in it, just like a walnut. It also seemed to have two distinct halves. Again, just like a walnut. What might he find inside if he cracked it open?

Pudge grabbed the thing, wrenched the lure free and readied to toss it overboard. Roxie swiped it out of his hands.

"And just what do you think you're doing?" she asked. She clung to the nut, like a quarterback guarding a football.

"It's junk. Lake junk. Just throw it back," said Pudge.

"Lake junk? I don't understand," Roxie said, shaking her head.

"People are always pulling old trash up from the bottom of the lake," Pudge said. "All sorts of crazy stuff. Machine parts, old bottles, stuff like that. My dad said never to mess with it. He said it could be dangerous."

Eddie's eyes were transfixed on the silver object. Slowly, he reached his hands out and, without a word, took the nut from Roxie's grasp. He stared at it like a magician staring into a crystal ball. There was something so familiar about the thing. The feel of the metal, the way that the sunlight...

"Oh no," said Pudge.

Startled, Eddie looked up. Pudge had risen and was staring off into the distance.

"What's wrong?" Eddie asked. But before Pudge could answer, Eddie saw the powerboat speeding toward them leaving a wild wake behind.

"Who is that?" asked Roxie as she stood to try to get a better view.

"It's the Mustache Mafia," Pudge moaned.

The powerboat roared toward them, siren bleeping, the sound of rock music blaring from the radio. It circled them once and cut its engines, the resulting wake setting *The Cheesy Breezy* rocking.

"Now, that's a boat," said Roxie.

"Quiet!" hissed Pudge.

Lance Eagan, a muscular teenager with a bad sunburn and an even worse mustache, stood up behind the wheel of the powerboat. His two buddies, who also sported wispy mustaches, stood behind him.

"Hey, Lance," said Pudge. "What's the haps?"

"You old enough to have a boating license, munch?" Lance asked. Whenever the guy talked, one side of his mustache lifted in a half snarl.

"You know I am. You wanna see it?" asked Pudge.

"Not necessary," said Lance with an unwarranted air of authority.

Eddie sat very still. Lance was trouble. His parents were rich and connected. Every summer they pulled strings to get Lance and his buddies Babcock and Hedges the cushy job of monitoring the lake. What it really meant was that Lance and company had free reign. To bully, to harass, to make life for other kids on the lake miserable.

"You know, one of your running lights is out," Lance huffed.

"Running lights?" Roxie asked, sneering. "How can you tell? It's daylight and he hasn't got them on."

Lance nodded to Babcock. The runt gingerly stepped from the powerboat over to Pudge's pontoon boat. He kicked at the aft running light, shattering it, sending bits of broken plastic into the water.

"You were saying?" Babcock hissed.

"You... you ignoramus!" Roxie sputtered.

Lance stared at her. "Who's this, your little girlfriend?"

Babcock and Hedges cackled maniacally. Pudge shot Roxie a glance, and there was fire in his eyes. The expression on his face said, "Let me handle this." He turned back to Lance and smiled.

"Maybe we can work this out. You guys hungry? I think I've got some coupons to my pop's place," he said. He began scrambling around the boat, searching through its different compartments. "Free pizza, free soda, free refills."

"Your dad's pizza is the worst. It tastes like roadkill," Babcock snickered.

"Yeah! Like roadkill pizza!" Hedges added gleefully.

Babcock shook his head at Hedges. "Shut up."

Finding a loose stack of coupons stuck in amongst the boats insurance paperwork, a triumphant Pudge rose, holding the coupons high.

"Who wants one?"

"What's that?" Lance asked. All eyes turned to the object in Eddie's lap. Eddie quickly moved it behind him.

"Nothing," Eddie said.

"Oooo! He's hiding something, Lance!" Hedges said, ever the master of the obvious.

"Hand it over," Lance said.

"It's mine," Eddie said, and the moment he said it, he knew it was true. The thing, whatever it was, *was* his, and he would protect it from anyone. Even from someone as intimidating as Lance.

Lance nodded to Hedges who quickly scrambled over to the pontoon boat. He grabbed the nut in his beefy hands. Eddie held on tight.

"Give over!" Hedges grunted.

"Not happening!" Eddie shouted, but he was losing his grip. In a couple of seconds, the oaf would have it.

The nut coughed.

Wisps of steam puffed out the sides. There was a sizzling sound, like hamburgers hitting the grill, and Hedges released his grip.

"Argh! He burned me! The little squirt burned me!" Hedges cried. He backed away from Eddie, tumbling back into the powerboat before thrusting his reddened hands into the lake. "Oooo-aahhh!" he sighed.

"What'd you do to him?" Lance sneered, his mustache twitching.

"N-nothing!" Eddie said. "I swear!"

Lance fumed. He turned to Pudge. "Toss me your tow line."

"Why?"

"Because I'm towing you in, munch," Lance growled.

Roxie stood. "On what grounds?"

"What?"

"On what grounds are you towing us in? Are we breaking any regulations? If so, please tell us which. And be specific. I want to be sure to give all the details to my father. He's a lawyer, you know. Civil cases, mostly. Liability, injury, that sort of thing. And so I repeat – on what grounds are you towing us in?"

Befuddled, Lance looked to his buddies. Babcock looked nervous, but Hedges steps forward to address Roxie's question.

"On the grounds that you better shut up!" piped up Hedges.

Lance glared at him. "Don't help me."

Suddenly the nut quivered in Eddie's hands. It let out an electric squeak. Instantly, the powerboat's engine surged and the boat lurched forward. Its bow collided with the pontoon boat, toppling the Mustache Mafia over each other.

"You... you... I'll...!" Lance sputtered, but before he could get his threat out, the powerboat roared to life once more, veering away from the island and off toward the distant shore. As the boat sped away, Eddie could still hear Hedges shrieking about his burned hands.

After a moment, Roxie spoke. "That was odd."

"Odd? That was downright weird," said Pudge. "Eddie, what the heck is that thing?"

Eddie looked down at the nut. "I don't know. But it seems to like me," said Eddie.

"It didn't scald you like it did that big ox, did it?" Roxie asked.

Eddie set the nut down between his feet and held out his hands. Nope. Not a burn to be seen.

"Yessir, downright weird," said Pudge.

"It's good to know your dad's a lawyer in case those jerks try to get back at us," said Eddie.

"Oh, he's not a lawyer."

"But you said..." said Eddie.

Roxie shrugged. "That's another thing you should know about me. I lie. A lot."

Pudge snorted, and soon all three of them were rolling with laughter.

"Did you see the look on Hedges' face when it burned him? I thought he was going to pee his swimsuit," Pudge cackled.

Eddie picked the nut back up. It was cold to the touch. He shook it. Nothing. Whatever juice had made it suddenly come to life had apparently drained away.

The peal of church bells sounded out from across the water. Six o'clock.

"I need to get home," said Roxie.

Pudge's face dropped. "But you said you'd help us figure out what to do for our science projects."

"I need to go."

"And I need a project!" Pudge whined.

"Don't worry. I'll text you some ideas later. Now, get this leaky bucket moving so I don't miss dinner."

"Fine," said Pudge. He turned the ignition, the engine sputtered to life and the pontoon boat slowly headed away from the island.

Roxie sidled up to Eddie. She didn't say anything, just stared down at the nut. Eddie sniffed the air. What was that smell?

"It's pine air freshener," said Roxie, freaking him out once again with her seemingly psychic ways. "My dad got me some perfume last Christmas, but it smells like old ladies. I prefer pine."

"It's... nice," lied Eddie.

"So, it looks like you've already got your science experiment figured out."

"How do you mean?" Eddie asked.

Roxie nodded to the nut. "If you can get it to do those whacky things again, you're a cinch to get an A. Call your project something like *The Mysterious Lake Nut* or *The Super-Nut-ural Wonder* or... I don't know. Something cool like that. Old Cupboard will flip."

"You think so?"

"I know so. Let me tell you a little secret about teachers. Most of them are bored out of their skulls. The substance of your project doesn't matter to them as long as you make it interesting. And that," she said, pointing at the nut, "is interesting."

"Doesn't help me none," Pudge mumbled.

"Quit your complaining. I've got three ideas that are guaranteed to get you at least a B," Roxie called back to him. "If you pick it up, pizza boy."

"B?" Pudge asked. "Picking it up, Roxanne Michael." He punched the throttle and the boat shuddered as it reached top speed.

"That's Michaels with an S! And it's Roxie, never Roxanne!" Roxie shouted over the roar of the engine. Pudge just laughed.

As the *Cheesy Breezy* made a beeline for the shore, the object in Eddie's lap made a single, plaintive bleep.

"What are you?" he wondered.

CHAPTER THREE

As Eddie approached his house, he noticed a new section of bare roof where the shingles had fallen away. It was directly above his bedroom window. He'd have to shimmy up there before the next big rain and patch it. The extra shingles he'd found in the garage were red and the rest of the roof was black, but shingles were shingles after all.

He looked around at the other houses on Mulberry Street. Neat, tidy homes with manicured lawns, yard gnomes and satellite dishes. He turned back to his own house. 734 Mulberry Street. Compared to the others, 734 Mulberry was a rotten apple.

He hopped off his bike, a second-hand deal his dad had brought back from one of his garage sale excursions, and headed for the front door, the nut secure in his backpack.

"Mom, I'm home..." He stopped short. The red light in the foyer was on. He sighed and took of his shoes. Red meant his mother was recording. Red meant he had to be quiet.

He tiptoed toward his room, which was through the living room, past the door to the basement and down the hall. How many times had he made it down the hall without letting the floorboards squeak underfoot? Three? Four? Maybe he'd be lucky today. Maybe...

SQUEAK!

He grimaced, lifted his offending foot off the offending floorboard and waited for the call from the basement he knew would surely come. And it did.

"Eddie!"

He'd done it now. He ruined her take. He might as well get to his room while the getting was good.

He slipped quickly into his bedroom where his old mutt Cooper lay waiting for him on his bed. As usual, Cooper had dragged some of his dirty clothes up onto the bed and had turned them into a nest of sorts. His tail thumped as he saw Eddie, but he didn't bark. The red light was on. Cooper knew better than to bark.

"Hey, boy," Eddie whisper and gave the pooch a scratch behind the ears. Cooper grunted with pleasure.

As soon as Eddie slipped off his backpack, the dog sat upright in bed. His eyes went wide and his lip curled back, showing his teeth. He let out a sound Eddie had never heard before.

"Cool it, Coop," Eddie said, but the dog was on high alert. He stared at Eddie's backpack like it was a predator invading his territory. He barked, and he wouldn't stop.

"Stop Cooper! Stop it, boy! Please!" begged Eddie, his voice struggling to remain a whisper and not quite doing it. "Hush, now. Hushhh!"

The sound of a door slamming in the basement stopped both Eddie and Cooper cold. Immediately, the dog leapt off the bed and scurried under it. Eddie closed his eyes and waited as he heard his mother coming up the stairs. He sat on the bed.

"Thanks a lot, Cooper," he grumbled.

Linda Edison poked her head into her son's room.

"I guess someone didn't see the red light," she said.

Eddie didn't look up. His eyes were on Cooper's tail sticking out from under the bed. His mother came into the room and sighed.

"I know it's not easy, Eddie. But I need to ask you again to please, please, please keep the noise down when I'm in my recording studio. I've got ten radio spots for the community college and three auditions to record. Things are starting to pick up, but that means I'm going to have to spend more time in the booth, so could you please..."

"Keep the noise down," Eddie said.

His mother walked over to him and sat next to him on the bed. She slumped against him and they just sat there for a while – two of a family of three.

"I'm sorry," his mother said.

"No, I'm sorry. I know you're working. I know we need the money. If Dad was here..."

His mother stopped him by putting her hand on his shoulder. Talking about his father, while being something they both sorely wanted to do, had a way of stopping them in their tracks. Talking about him always led to the same place – a dead end. No hope. No answers. No Dad.

"What commercials are you auditioning for?" he asked instead.

She smiled and said, "An antacid, an antidiuretic and a funeral home."

"Fun stuff," Eddie said.

His mother nudged Cooper's tail with her foot. He thumped it happily, enjoying the game. "Looks like someone's hiding from the wrath of Mom," she said.

"Once he heard you coming, he made a quick getaway. He's smarter than me," said Eddie.

Linda Edison rose. "I'd better get back to it. Can I have quiet for the next hour and a half? Would you mind doing that for me?"

"No problem, Mom."

"I love you," she said.

"Love you back."

As his mother turned, the thing in his backpack let out a slight electronic whoop. Just a little one, like something a smartphone might make when sending an email. She turned. "What was that?"

Eddie grabbed his backpack and muffled it under his arms. "Nothing."

"Well, try to keep *nothing* quiet, will you?"

"Sure thing, Mom."

Then she was gone. Eddie waited until he heard the basement door close, heard her footsteps disappear down into the basement. Then he relaxed back onto the bed.

The thing in the backpack warbled. Cooper growled underneath the bed.

Eddie stuck his head under the bed and said, "Okay, Coop. Time to go to your house."

Annoyed but resigned, Cooper crawled out from under the bed and trotted out the door and down the hall to his house, the dog crate in the guest room, where he wouldn't have to put up with warbling backpacks.

Eddie closed the door.

He carefully lifted the nut out of the pack. It was odd seeing it here in his room. It seemed unreal, yet here it was.

He set it on the bed and trained his desk lamp on it. A giant walnut. A giant *silver* walnut. From where? From outer space?

While having the answer might be nice, it would do him diddlysquat in Mr. Hubbard's class. He needed a science project idea to present by tomorrow morning, and he needed this nut to be it.

"Let's see what makes you tick."

Eddie opened a desk drawer, rummaged around and fished out his pocketknife. Another of Dad's garage sale finds. He'd said every boy needs a pocketknife. When Eddie had asked him what for, he'd simple answered, "For when you're in a pinch."

He flicked the knife open, the big broad blade shining in the lamplight, and attempted to slip the blade in the crease that delineated the two sections of the nut. As soon as the metal blade touched the metal nut, a jolt of electricity shot up his arm, across his chest, up his neck and his jaw clamped shut, almost catching his unsuspecting tongue.

"Whoa!" Eddie breathed as he tossed the knife aside. "Guess you didn't like that."

As he stared at the nut, a phrase popped into his head. Where he'd heard it, he hadn't a clue. *Fight fire with fire* was how the phrase went.

"Fire? What in the...?" Then it hit him. Electricity! *Fight electricity with electricity.*

Eddie quickly took inventory of the room. The lamp. Should he cut its cord, strip the wires, using them as some sort of defibrillator to shock the thing into opening? No. Common household current was only common in name - he knew from a failed attempt to rewire his mom's vacuum cleaner what a wallop common household current could pack.

"Lawnmower!" Eddie thought.

Instead of attempting the trek down the squeaky hallway, Eddie opened his bedroom window and crawled out instead. Once in the front yard, he dashed around to the side of the house where he kept the lawnmower. While it wasn't ancient, it wasn't new. Just new enough to be the self-starter type with a...

"Battery!" Eddie said as he yanked the lawnmower's innards out.

Soon, he was back in his room, his hands covered in oil, the grimy battery sitting on the bed next to the nut. Eddie grabbed hold of the two cables leading from the battery and held them gingerly on either side of the object.

"Here goes nothing," he hummed.

He brought the cables into contact with the shiny metal surface. The cables gave off a shower of sparks, smoke rose, the smell of burning metal filled the room.

When the smoke had cleared, the nut remained untouched. "Yup, 'nothing' is right," Eddie said.

***

After his mother had finished recording her auditions, Eddie set about laying a tarp over the bare patch on the roof. It would have to do in case they got rain before he was able to lay down the new shingles. And from the angry look of the sky, that rain could come sooner than later.

By the time he was done, his mother had dinner ready. Microwave dinners seemed to be on the menu more and more these days, but Eddie didn't complain. Mom had a lot on her mind.

It was around nine o'clock when he finally headed back to his room, dreading the thought of going to school the next day. What would he say when Mr. Hubbard called on him to present his project? A hundred scenarios played out in his mind, none of them good.

He decided to call Pudge and see how he was getting along.

"Hey Eddie. S'up?"

"Just working on my presentation. How's yours going?"

"I'm all set, dude. That Roxie may be a weird one, but she gave me a killer idea. You know how my pop's pizza is so greasy?"

"Greasiest in town."

"Be quiet. Well, she said I should come up with a new kind of plate just for pizza. A plate that drinks up all the grease. Pretty cool, huh?"

Eddie gulped. Even Pudge had his idea down. "So... you're all ready for tomorrow?"

"Heck, I was ready two hours ago. I'm watching *Bee Tornado*. You seen it yet? Man, I hate bees!"

Eddie let Pudge get back to his movie. He walked over to where the nut was perched on the bed and set it down in the closet. "I'll deal with you later," he said and closed the door.

He flopped back down on the bed. A rumble of thunder threatened the night. Concentrate, Edison! Time to brainstorm. What do you want to work on? How about... or what if... or maybe I could...

Before the next roll of thunder, Eddie's eyes closed and he dropped to sleep.

A tremendous flash of lighting woke Eddie with a start. He sat up in bed and looked around the room. It was pitch dark. The power must be out. How long had he been asleep?

"Mom?" he called, but Mom was on the other side of the house, and after a long day of recording she'd be out like a light. Out like all the lights.

He felt a drop of water hit his forehead and he peered upward. He clicked on his phone and raised it above his head, letting its screen light up the ceiling. In the dim glow, he could see a brown stain spreading across the ceiling, bubbling the paint.

He heard a flapping sound outside, quickly opened the window and stuck out his head. The rain pelted his face, and in the next flash of lightning he saw the tarp hanging from the gutter. The bare patch on the roof must be right above his head.

"Great," he sighed. Nothing to do about it now. He wasn't about to crawl up on the roof at night with lightning dancing all around him. Instead he shut the window, searched out his wastebasket and placed it under the leak.

He grabbed his pillow and plopped down on the floor, pulling an afghan off the chair and wrapping it around himself.

It was then that he noticed that the closet door was open.

Before he could turn his phone's light on, something leapt out of the corner and landed on his chest, knocking the wind out of him. It was too dark to see what it was, but Eddie could guess. The next streak of lightning illuminated the room, confirming his fear.

The silver nut was standing on his chest.

Somehow, the thing had sprouted spindly, telescoping legs from the grooves in its skin. It swayed over him like a metallic spider. Eddie tried to cry out for his mother, but the appearance of the nut had robbed him of his voice.

Eddie tried to roll to his side, to knock the thing loose, but little claws on the ends of its legs dug into his shirt, into his skin. It smarted like a prick from a fishhook. Eddie yelped and lay back again.

The nut started humming. Low at first, almost unnoticeable with the sound of thunder rumbling outside. Then a sliver of green light appeared in the nut's skin. It was opening, splitting apart, a ghastly glow spilling out from inside.

Through slitted eyes, Eddie watched as the nut opened like a clam. A miniature, firestorm raged at its center – sparks, flashing lights, flickering arcs of electricity. The thing leaned in, directing its chaotic innards toward his face.

In the midst of the mayhem, a calm voice addressed him from inside the nut.

"Say cheese," it said. Then Eddie's world erupted in an explosion of light.

Chapter Four

Eddie bolted upright. Sunlight hit him in the face and he winced. Morning? How could it be morning?

He quickly looked around for the nut and found it lying on the floor next to him. Or at least what was left of it. The thing was open, its little legs curled up, its inner workings as charred and lifeless as a dead campfire. He gave the thing a little kick. No reaction. Whatever it used to be, it was now nothing more than junk.

"Unreal," he thought as he rubbed his forehead. He stood and was rewarded with a massive headache. The kind you get when you eat ice cream too fast. He shook his head to try to clear it.

An eruption of numbers filled his mind, swirling around in a great cloud. As soon as he stopped moving his head, the cloud went still and the digits began to drop away, like bits of plastic snow in a snow globe.

Eddie felt woozy and was afraid he was about to upchuck right then and there, but the feeling soon subsided. He spied his phone lying on the carpet, grabbed it and groggily sat on the edge of his bed.

He glanced over at his clock. It was flashing 12:00 at him over and over. Oh, yeah. The power had gone out, hadn't it? He turned on his phone to get the right time and...

It was 10:15. The school day had started almost an hour and a half ago. Not only was he late, he was *really* late.

He scrambled around the room to find his socks and shoes. Why hadn't Mom woken him up? Her alarm clock must have fallen prey to the power outage as well. Rats! Of all the days to be late – the day old Hubbard expected them to present their ideas for their final projects.

Eddie froze. Final projects! What was he going to do? His only possible project lay in the middle of the floor in pieces.

There was no time to stand around feeling sorry for himself. Eddie rushed for the door and was down the hallway and through the foyer in the blink of an eye.

"Time to wake up, Mom! Can you feed Cooper? I'm late!" he shouted toward his mother's bedroom as he dashed out the door, grabbed his bike and started pedaling like a maniac down Mulberry Street.

Trees and houses whipped by as Eddie sped onward. His mind raced almost as fast as his bike. He tried to turn his focus toward coming up with a last minute idea to satisfy old Hubbard, but his thoughts kept returning to last night's storm, the silver nut and the jumble of numbers whirling around in his brain.

"A bad dream. It was just a bad dream," he tried to convince himself, but he knew better. He had to tell Pudge and Roxie about it. Maybe if they all put their heads together, they could figure out what had happened.

Dad. If Dad were here, he'd figure it out. If Dad were here, he'd figure out a lot of things. Like how to keep the roof from leaking, how to make sure Mom didn't kill herself working so hard, how...

His front tire hit a fallen branch, and he flew over the handlebars, hit the asphalt and came to a skidding stop in the bushes along the side of the road.

"Get it together, Edison," he told himself. "Get it together."

Twenty minutes later, he pulled up in front of Lakeview School. He rushed his bike into the bike rack and ran toward the side entrance. He grabbed the door handle and gave it a tug. Locked.

Oh, no, he thought, he'd have to go in the main entrance. That meant going past the office. That meant going past Principal Wood.

The sound of squealing brakes caught his ear, and he peeked around the corner. Pulling up to the entrance to the lunchroom was a small delivery truck with words *Bunches o' Lunches* stenciled across its side.

Without thinking, Eddie made a dash for the truck. As he sprinted across the playground, he passed the first floor classrooms. He kept his eyes on the truck even though he could feel kids' eyes staring at him through the windows.

He reached the truck just as a burly man was opening up the back. Eddie skidded to a halt.

"I'm here!" he said, breathing heavily.

The man turned and stared at him. "Yeah? So?" he asked.

"I'm your student aid. To help deliver the food? I'm getting credit in social studies by helping you. I'm really psyched to learn everything I can about the service industry."

The man cocked his head at Eddie. "No one told me nuthin' about it. But then again, nobody tells me nuthin' about nuthin'. Come on."

He brought down the first of the food delivery carts and passed it off to Eddie.

"This goes to the kitchen. Once you're done with that..."

"The kitchen! Got it!" Eddie said, and before the man could finish his instructions, Eddie was steering the cart toward the kitchen.

"Be careful!" the man called after him. "There are taco shells in there!"

Eddie raced the cart to the kitchen. He failed to stop in time to keep the cart from slamming into the wall, startling Mrs. Whitman, an elderly woman in a hairnet. Inside, he heard the taco shells crunch.

"Here you go, Mrs. Whitman!" he said. "Happy Taco Tuesday! Gotta get back to class!" And with that, Eddie ran for the door.

Luckily, the hall was empty. As he made his way toward his classroom, he heard the murmur of teachers and students in other rooms. It was weird being in the hallway while everyone else was inside. But ever since the nut woke up last night, weird seemed to be the new normal.

He reached Mr. Hubbard's room and peeked inside. Jimmy Ticks was at the front of the class, his hands fluttering nervously.

"And... and then I'm going to put the seeds into paper cups and... and I'll feed some of them water and... and I'll feed some of them root beer and... and... and..."

Jimmy was bombing, but at least he had a project to present. Eddie had been so focused on getting to his classroom unnoticed that the reality of walking into class with nothing to present hadn't sunk in. He was thinking that maybe he should have had his mom call him in sick when Mr. Hubbard poked his head out the door. They were face to face.

"Please join us, Mr. Edison," Mr. Hubbard hissed.

Eddie gulped. Being this close to the crusty, old teacher he could finally confirm what every student had long suspected: Mr. Hubbard wore a toupee. No way that hair was real.

The other students snickered as Eddie scurried to his seat. Jimmy Ticks took this as his cue to start up again.

"And as soon as the plants begin to grow..."

"Yes, yes, that will do. Another plant project. Thrilling. That will be our fifth, will it not?" sneered Hubbard. Jimmy hiccupped and snuck back to his seat.

A wave of hope swept over Eddie. Perhaps Mr. Hubbard was going to let his tardiness slide.

"If *I* was going to come up with a project, I think I would explore the concept of time." Mr. Hubbard stalked about the room. "How some people respect other's time and some don't. Any thoughts, Mr. Edison?"

The teacher stopped directly over Eddie. Looking up at him, Eddie thought he could detect where Mr. Hubbard's real hair ended and the fake stuff began.

"I'm sorry I was late. I was..." he started to say, but before he could finish, Roxie jumped up from her desk, her backpack in hand. She was wearing the same ratty sweater as the day before.

"I'm ready to present my project idea, Mr. Hubbard. You'll have to excuse me, but I'm so excited I just can't wait!"

Pudge laughed, then caught himself as Hubbard looked his way. Caught off guard, the teacher simply waved to Roxie to proceed. He walked back to his desk and sat down, popping a Diet Carney Cola can and slurping loudly over Roxie's presentation.

"Has anyone in this room heard of the Jersey Devil?" Instantly, Roxie had everyone's attention. "Well? That wasn't a rhetorical question, people," said Roxie. "Has anyone heard about the Jersey Devil?"

A dozen voices rang out. "It's a monster!"

"Like Bigfoot!"

"Only its got wings!"

"And it lives in New Jersey!"

"So the story goes," said Roxie. "The creature, said to be part horse, part goat, part winged beast, has terrorized residents of New Jersey for ages."

The class was hanging on her every word.

"It is my contention that the Jersey Devil is no myth. And, if my project is approved..." She glanced over at Mr. Hubbard. "... I shall set about to prove its existence."

Eddie shivered as he watched the odd girl. Weird was definitely the new normal.

He looked at Hubbard – he was paying rapt attention. He guessed Roxie was right about teachers.

Dazzle them with a mysterious monster story after a string of boring old projects and they'll perk right up.

"Very well. Have at it. Only make sure that you don't sensationalize your subject. Stick to the facts and the facts only, you hear me, Ms. Michael?"

"That's Michaels with an..."

Mr. Hubbard turned his focus to Eddie. "You're up, Mr. Edison." Eddie's stomach did a backflip. He didn't move. "Come on, I want to get this over before the next ice age. Chop, chop!"

Eddie rose to his feet. Roxie threw him a sympathetic look. He glanced quickly to where Pudge sat with the diagram of his newfangled pizza plate. His buddy mouthed, "You ready?" Eddie shook his head. Not even close.

As Eddie walked to the front of the room, he thought, "*So, this is what it feels like to step in front of a firing squad.*"

He stopped next to Mr. Hubbard's desk and turned to face the class. A roomful of expectant faces met his. He opened his mouth.

"I..."

Mr. Hubbard sighed. Another presentation going down in flames. What else did he expect from Eddie? He crumpled his empty soda can and aimed at the wastebasket.

"You should recycle that," said Jimmy Ticks. Mr. Hubbard just shook his head, and tossed the can into the air.

Eddie's hand shot out and grabbed it in midflight.

He looked at the can in his hand in disbelief. Had he meant to do that? If so, why? What possible use could Hubbard's old can be to him?

No sooner had he asked himself the question than the answer burst into his head. With nothing else to offer, he decided to run with it.

"Jimmy's right," Eddie said. "We should recycle this." He dropped the can on the floor and smashed it flat with his foot.

"Enough stalling," Hubbard warned.

"Oh, I'm not stalling. It's just that I need..." And in a flash, he knew exactly what he needed. He pulled his phone from his pocket and dropped it on the floor as well and crushed it underfoot. The entire class winced, instinctively grabbing for their own phones, wherever they had them hidden away.

Eddie dropped to his knees and began scrounging around in the wreckage of his phone.

"Sometimes the stuff we throw away can be more interesting than we ever would have imagined," he said.

"Is there a point to all this carnage?" asked Hubbard.

Eddie ignored him, searching frantically for... there! That little bit there with the wires coming out of each end. He wrapped the wire through the cans flip-top, attaching the two items, and then scanned the room with his eyes.

"All we have to do is to look at things in a different way." Bingo! His eyes lit upon the intercom speaker hanging on the wall next to the door. He rushed over to it, grabbed it and pulled it down, ripping the speaker from the wall. It gave a squeal and was silent.

"I've had quite enough of your antics!" said Mr. Hubbard. "Go to Mr. Wood's office."

Eddie focused on his task, his hands moving like lightning as they stripped the intercom apart, twisting wires, bending strips of metal, attaching the soda can...

"*Now,* Mr. Edison!" Eddie's hands stopped and he held the patchwork device out in front of him, a proud look on his face. "And voilà!" Eddie cried, and he connected the last two wires.

Whump! A shockwave echoed out of the device in Eddie's hands. Eddie could feel it in his chest and he could tell that the rest of the class felt it too. The windows trembled and the toupee on Mr. Hubbard's head lifted slightly.

Then, everything went still.

Mr. Hubbard rose from his desk, his face red with anger. "Since you have chosen to ignore me, I'll walk you down to the office myself."

Eddie shook his device. He didn't understand. He could see it working in his mind's eye. What had gone wrong?

Suddenly, his creation shuddered to life. It gave off a thumping sound like the bass beat of a song. The air in front of Eddie began to shimmer, to bubble. Soon, it was swirling like water circling a drain.

"He's making a storm!" someone cried. "He's making a tornado!" said another.

Roxie stood, amazed at what she was seeing. "No. He's making a black hole."

Eddie grinned wide as the swirling mass grew stronger and stronger. It *was* a black hole. And *he* had made it! He was going to get an A for sure. Heck, he was probably going to get an A+. There was no way that old man Hubbard would be able to deny him the top grade in the class.

That was when Mr. Hubbard's toupee ripped free from the top of his head.

If there was ever anything that could steal focus from a miniature black hole appearing in the middle of a group of fifth graders, it was the sudden disappearance of their teacher's hair. The class gasped, and Mr. Hubbard shrieked as his toupee sailed across the room and plunged down the black hole's throat and disappeared with a poof of hair.

The black hole vanished.

Mr. Hubbard quickly covered his bald head with his hands as the lunch bell sounded. The class bolted for the door, and Eddie took cover in their numbers and moved with them, fleeing for the safety of the lunchroom.

"Single file, single file!" Mr. Hubbard yelled after them, but no one listened.

As Eddie moved with the herd toward the lunchroom, a voice inside his head whispered, "Tonight... tonight... tonight..." It was the same voice that had appeared when the nut had come to life.

"Tonight..."

CHAPTER FIVE

During lunch, Eddie had tried talk to Pudge and Roxie, but the table was abuzz with conversations about Hubbard's hairpiece and complaints about how all the taco shells were broken.

When Eddie and his classmates had returned to the classroom, Ms. Lee, the morning kindergarten teacher, was waiting for them. She explained that Mr. Hubbard had taken ill and would be returning tomorrow. But lucky for them, she had her guitar with her.

After three hours of singing songs and listening to stories about Ms. Lee's cats, the final bell rang and Eddie and his classmates were free.

Pudge and Roxie caught up with him in the hall. "Come on," said Pudge. "We're going to Pop's."

A few minutes later, they were sitting in a booth at Pudge's father's pizza joint, Pop's Pizzeria, a little paneled restaurant overlooking Lake Mohawk. Pudge's dad was larger than life. He was usually in a great mood, singing with the radio, joking with the customers, but today, he set the plain pie and drinks in front of Pudge and his friends without saying a word.

"Thanks, Pop," said Pudge. Eddie and Roxie echoed his thanks.

"Fugetaboutit," Pop said and turned to leave.

"Something wrong?" Pudge asked. Pop considered this for a moment and then motioned for his son to scooch over in the booth.

"What's this I hear about you getting into it with Lance and his crew?"

"What? Who said we got into it?" Pudge already had his first slice in hand but at this he set it down.

"I got a call from his father. He told me that you and Eddie and..." He looked across to where Roxie was sitting shaking a tremendous amount of Parmesan cheese onto her pizza. "Who's the new girl?"

"That's Roxie, Pops. She's okay. What did Lance's father say?"

"He said you were mouthing off to Lance and his guys. Being real wisenheimers. He also said that a boy got burned." Pop looked serious now. "Can you tell me anything about that?"

"We weren't mouthing off and we weren't being wisenheimers," said Pudge. "Whatever those are."

"Weisenheimers," said Roxie, pizza sauce dripping out of the side of her mouth. "Smart alecks, wisecrackers..."

"Those guys had it in for us. And as for the burns," Eddie said, "that guy Hedges brought it on himself. I pulled something out of the lake, he tried to take it away and somehow the thing burned him. That's the honest truth, Mr. Rizzotti."

Pop scratched his chin and considered Eddie. Then he turned back to Pudge. "What'd I tell you about that lake junk."

"Throw it back," Pudge said.

"That's right. Well, for what it's worth, I believe you. I'm pretty sure Lance's father is expecting us to call back with an apology, but I think I'll just let it sit for a while. He'll probably cancel his weekly order to his office, but hey." He looked at Roxie. "We've got new customers coming in every day, right?"

Pudge laughed, relieved. His father rose and leaned in. "But I think we should let *The Cheesy Breezy* sit for a while too."

"What?" Pudge looked wounded.

"Just until this thing blows over. I'll let you know when you can take her out again. Enjoy your pie." With that, Pop headed back to the kitchen.

Pudge grabbed his slice and stuffed it in his mouth. "Not fair," he mumbled between chews.

Roxie shook her head. "Eddie whipped up a black hole, almost sending us hurtling after old Cupboard's wig and you're worried about a nautical time out?"

"That was some strange stunt you pulled, Edison," Pudge said. "How'd you pull it off?"

Eddie shrugged. "I have no idea. Once I grabbed the aluminum can, my mind started putting all the pieces together for me. Ever since that thing I pulled out of the water crawled on top of me and shot me full of electricity, I feel... different."

"Whoa! Hold up!" said Pudge. "It did what? When were you going to tell us that?"

"That's a pretty big detail to leave out," Roxie agreed.

"And then there's that voice," Eddie said.

"What voice?" asked Pudge. He was clearly about ready to throttle Eddie.

"I think it's a man's voice, but since I'm only hearing it in my head, I'm really not sure."

"What did it say?" Roxie asked.

"Tonight."

"What about tonight?"

"That's all it said. *Tonight.* But the voice kept repeating, echoing over and over again. What do you think that means?"

"It echoed? Maybe someone's trying to tell you that your head is hollow," Pudge said and cupped his hands around his mouth. "Hello... hello... hello..."

Roxie elbowed him in the ribs. "Or maybe it's an invitation," she said as she looked out the window at the lake.

"I don't follow," said Eddie.

Roxie looked at the two boys as if she was dealing with three-year-olds. "Tonight... tonight... tonight...? Echo... echo...?"

Eddie looked at Pudge, and the answer clicked for both of them at the same time. "Echo Island!"

"If you want to get to the bottom of this, you're going to have to go back to Echo Island tonight," said Roxie.

"What do you mean me? If I'm going, you're going, right? Both of you," said Eddie.

"You're asking me to disobey my pop," said Pudge. He shifted in his seat.

"Come on, Pudge. Please," Eddie pleaded.

Pop stepped away from the kitchen. The phones were ringing off the hook. "Phil," he called to Pudge, "that new McCarthy kid just called in sick. I'm going to need you to give me a hand."

"But Pop!"

"No buts, wise guy. Finish up and say bye to your friends. The dinner rush is on!"

Pudge took one last bite of pizza and got up. "Okay," he said. "But if we get caught..."

"We won't get caught, Pudge," Eddie said. "I promise."

Pudge looked to Roxie. "You're on board too?"

She smiled. "Aye aye, Captain *Phil*."

"Don't call me that," Pudge growled and headed back to the kitchen.

Eddie looked across at Roxie. She stared back at him. She didn't say a word, just kept staring at him with that pine air freshener scent of hers. He nibbled on his pizza. Oh boy, thought Eddie. He hoped she didn't think this was a date. This wasn't a date. Was it?

He got so nervous that he blurted out, "So, you're doing your project on the Jersey Devil?"

"You know I am," she said. She wouldn't unlock eyes with him. She seemed to like to see him squirm. Finally, she broke off.

"You want to know something funny?" she asked. Eddie shrugged. "The last reported sighting was right here in Lake Mohawk. At the Turtle Cove Diner."

Eddie froze. Turtle Cove Diner. Why wasn't he surprised to hear Roxie mention the name of the diner where his father went missing?

***

Roxie joined him for part of the bike ride home.

She rode a black ten speed with no working brakes, as far as he could see.

"When I went to the library last night to research my project, I hadn't planned on doing it on the Jersey Devil. I wanted to study the effects of different kinds of music on Venus flytraps."

"Mr. Hubbard would have *loved* that. Another plant project," Eddie said as he pedaled madly to make it up the steep hill.

"While I was sitting at a table flipping through some books, this old man who was sitting next to me reading a newspaper suddenly flipped out," said Roxie. "He threw down his paper and started yelling at the top of his lungs. This old woman, I'm pretty sure she was his wife, had to take him outside to calm him down."

"What was he yelling about?"

Roxie launched into an amazing imitation of an old man. "What are they thinking?" she shouted. "The Devil will get them. The Jersey Devil will get them all!"

"What did he look like? This old guy?" Eddie asked.

"Like a regular old guy, I guess. He was wearing a heavy flannel coat and it was a hot day. Weird."

Eddie looked over at Roxie as she powered on to the top of the hill, her ratty sweater flapping in the warm breeze, but he didn't say anything about it. Old guy, heavy flannel coat. That sounded like Abel Sparks, his parents' old friend.

"Well, after his wife took him outside I walked over and picked up the newspaper he'd dropped. Right in the middle of the page he had been looking at was an ad for the Turtle Cove Diner. *Grand Reopening* it said."

They had reached the top of the hill and were just starting down. Eddie worried about Roxie's lack of brakes.

"I went outside and started talking to them. The woman wanted me to go away, but the old man just kept going on and on about the monster. 'You believe me, don't you?' he asked me, and I swore I did. Then his wife took him away."

"Is that it?" Eddie asked.

"Not quite!" Roxie shouted as she started to speed past Eddie.

"What else?" called Eddie. By this point, Roxie was almost to the bottom of the hill. How was she going to slow down before she hit the sharp curve?

"Hold on... *whoo-hoo!*" Roxie hooted as she reached the bottom of the hill.

Just before she hit the gravel that would have sent most bicyclists skidding into a world of hurt, Roxie purposely hit a mound of dirt at the side of the road and her bike leapt into the air. She twisted the bicycle gracefully and came down sideways on both tires, kicking up a shower of rocks.

She came to a complete stop. Eddie was so impressed that he almost forgot to brake himself. He came to a halting stop right next to her.

"Here." Roxie pulled a torn piece of newspaper from her pocket and handed it to him.

"What is it?"

"An article I looked up after I met the old man," said Roxie.

Eddie looked at the ripped paper. "You took this from the library?"

"That's another thing you should know about me," she said.

"You steal things?"

"Only from libraries."

Eddie looked at the paper. *Fire Destroys Turtle Cove Diner.* There wasn't much of a story. Just a quick blurb about the fire and how two people had been rescued from the flames but how two were still missing: a waitress working the late shift and a man named...

"William Edison," Eddie read aloud. His voice shook almost as much as his hands. He knew the story as a story, but seeing it in black and white made it way too real.

"I didn't understand when old Cupboard said your father disappeared," said Roxie, "but now I think I do. I think your father was taken by the..."

"I gotta get home," Eddie said quickly and tossed the article back to her. It was too much. It was way too much. He turned his bike and started pedaling toward home.

"Wait!" Roxie called after him. "I'm sorry. I didn't mean to upset you."

"That's okay," Eddie said over his shoulder.

"Are we still going tonight?"

"Maybe," he called back to her as he zipped away. "Maybe."

***

Eddie lay on his bed, looking down at the floor. Where he had last seen the remains of the silver nut there was now only a pile of dust. He'd have to clean it up, get rid of it, but for now he just stared at it.

It was almost midnight and no Pudge, no Roxie. Maybe they'd decided to leave him alone.

He was a bit disappointed but also relieved. He wanted things to go back to normal. But what was normal? He couldn't even remember any more. Every time he let his mind wander, a whirlwind of information filled his head. Diagrams of inventions he'd never even seen, answers to equations he'd never tried to solve. Numbers, symbols, formulae and theories, all jumbled around in his noggin, fighting for his attention.

And what the heck was 'string theory'?

He rolled over and tried to push it all from his mind. Cooper lay next to him on the bed looking concerned.

He licked Eddie's face – a slobbery, wet kiss that smelled like dog treats.

"You're lucky, Coop," Eddie sighed. "All you have to worry about is when your next meal is."

A pebble hit the window, and Cooper snapped his head around, growling. When Pudge's face appeared on the other side of the glass the dog started wiggling with happy recognition.

Pudge stared in at Eddie. He mouthed, "Are we on or what?"

Roxie appeared next to Pudge, a lit flashlight in hand. Eddie guessed he could just pull the shade down, and they'd get the hint that he didn't want to go any further. That they should drop it.

Instead, he leaned over and opened the window. "I'll be right out," he said.

CHAPTER SIX

The surface of Lake Mohawk was still, its surface like glass as *The Cheesy Breezy* slowly chugged toward Echo Island. Pudge had the running lights off and was piloting by memory. Eddie hoped his memory was good.

He sat perched at the bow of the boat. He didn't want to miss a thing. The trouble was there was no moon that night, and they sailed in nearly pitch blackness. Only the scattered lights from the shoreline gave Eddie any sense of where they were.

"You do this often?" Roxie asked Pudge. "Sail blind?"

"Nothing to it," Pudge said smugly.

Eddie could see the empty house silhouetted up ahead. There was still time to turn back.

The boat lurched suddenly, and Eddie almost toppled over the edge.

"Rock," said Pudge. "Sorry."

"Thought you said there was nothing to it," Roxie snorted. Pudge waved her off.

"Roxie, hand me your flashlight," Eddie said. Roxie passed it to him and he flipped it on, scanning the shoreline. "There's an old dock off to your right, Pudge."

"*Starboard*, you mean," said Pudge. Roxie rewarded him with a smack to the back of his head. "Ow!"

Pudge guided the puttering pontoon boat toward the wooden dock, slowing as he went. Once he was close, he cut the motor and let the boat slide up next to the dock.

"Tie us off, Eddie," said Pudge.

Eddie stepped off the boat and onto the dock. As soon as he did so, the rotten wood gave way beneath his feet and he plunged into the water below.

As he struggled upward, he managed to keep a hold on the flashlight. When he breached the surface, the beam caught a wide-eyed Roxie in the face.

"You okay?" she asked.

"Never better," he said sarcastically. "Help me up."

After Roxie and Pudge pulled Eddie from the water, they agreed they should jump for the shore rather than risk treading on the rickety dock again. Roxie was first, and she made a good show of it. Only her mismatched sneakered feet got wet.

Eddie went next, but the weight of his wet clothes kept him from doing his best. He landed knee-deep in the water and had to wade the rest of the way.

"Maybe I should try out for track and field next year," Roxie gloated. Eddie rolled his eyes at her.

It was Pudge's turn. He looked down at the water with trepidation. "I think someone should stay with the boat," he said. "As a lookout."

"A lookout?" Roxie frowned. "What are you going to lookout for? It's almost one in the morning."

"All the same..." Pudge started to say, but trailed off.

Eddie nodded. "You hang here. Roxie and I will scope things out." He headed into the brush, Roxie at his heels.

"Why isn't he coming with us?" Roxie huffed.

"If you haven't noticed, Pudge isn't the most... athletic guy around."

"So?"

"I think he was embarrassed to try to make the jump," said Eddie.

"Embarrassed about what?"

Eddie stopped and shined the flashlight in Roxie's face. "About you. He didn't want you to see him if he fell. Me? He wouldn't give a lick. But you?"

Roxie considered this. "That's actually kind of sweet. No one ever cares what I think. Poor guy. Should I go back and tell him...?"

"No."

"But I just want to tell him that he doesn't have to be..."

"Do you want to find out why we've been invited here tonight or not?" asked Eddie as he walked on toward the house. Things were always more complicated when you added girls into the mix. They always wanted to talk about feelings and stuff. Maybe he should have left Roxie back on the boat instead of Pudge.

Roxie looked back toward Pudge one last time and then scampered to catch up. "What do you think we should be looking for?" she asked.

"I haven't the foggiest," Eddie said. "But I'm hoping that we know it when we see it."

The house loomed up in front of them. Eddie scanned it with the flashlight. It was covered in graffiti and vines.

"Hello?" Eddie pushed on the front door. It creaked, fell off its hinges and toppled to the floor. As they entered, Eddie realized it was only a house in theory. The outer walls of the structure remained more or less intact, but the inside of the place was gutted. A fire perhaps?

"I was the one who brought the flashlight, you know," said Roxie as she snatched it out of Eddie's hand. She pointed it upward toward the ceiling. Or at least where the ceiling used to be. The beam reached all the way up to the second floor and beyond. The light revealed the rafters and the roof. The roof was open in spots to reveal the night sky.

"Hello?" Eddie repeated. The only response was the hoot of an owl, annoyed at having been disturbed.

"You sure the voice said tonight?" Roxie asked.

"I'm sure. Actually that's all it said," said Eddie.

The two of them searched as much of the house as they could, alternating who got to use the flashlight. Some sections threatened to come tumbling down on them as soon as they stepped onto the floorboards, and they backed off. Finally, when they had searched every inch of the place, Eddie stopped. Nothing. No mysterious figure to welcome him, no disembodied voice to urge him on. Nothing. Eddie shook his head. What else should he have expected?

He handed Roxie the flashlight. "I don't see anything, do you?"

"Not yet. But maybe we aren't looking close enough." She moved the flashlight beam around the main room. It glanced off a crumbling staircase, a ruined table and chairs. "Tell me what you see."

"That's silly," Eddie said.

"Do it."

"All right," said Eddie. "I spy with my little eye..."

"Be serious," Roxie groaned.

Eddie sighed. "I see a broken window. I see peeling wallpaper."

"Go on."

"I see a moldy old sofa. I see..." He stopped and squinted his eyes.

What had happened to the wallpaper? A moment ago it was cracked and hanging off the wall. Now it was back up, no longer faded but a vibrant green.

"What?" crowed Roxie. "You see *what*?"

The shattered window had somehow repaired its glass. What was going on?

Eddie heard a chirping noise and looked down. Two yellow, blinking eyes peered at Eddie from behind a remarkably restored bookcase. He swiped the flashlight out of Roxie's hands and trained it on the eyes.

A metal frog stared up at him. Its skin was polished green chrome. Its yellow eyes ogled him and it burbled, "*Rej-jip.*"

"What is that?" Eddie asked.

"What's what?"

"*Rej-JIP!*" the frog-thing shrieked. It leapt into the air, straight for Eddie's head.

With a gasp, Eddie dropped the flashlight, put his hands out to shield himself from the leaping creature and...

He disappeared. Even before the flashlight hit the ground. "Eddie?" Roxie called. "Eddie?!?"

Eddie caught the metal frog a split second before it landed on his face. Its mouth opened and closed on squeaky hinges as it croaked, "*Rej-jip! Rej-jip! Rehhhj-jip!*"

"I see you've met Reggie," a voice behind Eddie said. It was the same voice he'd heard before.

Eddie whirled around, holding the squirming metal frog at arm's length, its clockwork innards spinning and clicking.

Standing at a workbench piled high with spools of wire, salvaged radio parts and gutted laptop computers was a lanky man in a wrinkled lab coat. His hair was an uncombed bird's nest, his eyes wild and bright. To Eddie's mind, the man looked quite mad.

"Come here, Reggie!" the man called. The metal frog wriggled out of Eddie's hands, hit the floor with a clank and hopped over to the workbench. It vaulted up into the air and landed on a broken toaster. "Funny little fellow. I've packed him full of memory but I still can't get him to say *ribbit*. Can I, Reggie?"

On cue, the frog said, "*Rej-jip!*"

"Who... where...?" Eddie was at a loss for words. He twirled about, taking in the room around him. It seemed to be half living quarters, half laboratory. No longer was the old house... well, old. It was antiquey, no question about it, but it was no longer crumbling down around him. The ceiling was back in place and electric lights blazed in wall sconces around the room.

Piles of machine parts littered every corner – disassembled vacuum cleaners, DVD players, microwave ovens, lawnmowers, TVs. It was like someone emptied an entire junk shop into the place.

"Look at you, you're all wet. Stay clear of those cables on the ground. Don't want you to electrocute yourself before we get started," said the man, as he walked over to a chalkboard and started wiping it clean of the mathematical formulae covering every inch of its surface. "We have *a lot* of ground to cover."

"What... who...?" Eddie continued to stammer. The man turned back to him, seemingly surprised at his confusion.

"Am I moving too fast?" asked the man. "I always do that. Bad habit of mine. Introductions first, eh? Best way to start things off. All right... you. You are Edward J. Edison but you go by Eddie. You live on Mulberry Street with your mother and your loyal dog Cooper. You attend Lakeview Elementary School and you are deathly afraid of clowns. Your turn."

Eddie's confusion quickly morphed into anger. "What do you mean, my turn? I have no idea who you are!" He was shaking.

The man smiled and shook his head. "I'm sorry. Of course, I've spent a little too much time on my own these past few years, and I think my social skills must be a bit rusty."

The man leapt forward with his hand out. Eddie recoiled in fear.

"Names. Yes, names. Yours is Eddie, as we've established. Mine is... that's a bit tricky isn't it? Well, I suppose for the sake of this conversation, why don't you call me... Mesmer."

Eddie looked at the man's outstretched hand. "Mesmer? That's your name?"

"Not in the slightest." The man took Eddie's hand in his and shook it firmly. "It's so very, very good to meet you. And a bit odd too, I must confess. But still, a pleasure. A profound pleasure."

It was all too much for Eddie. His head was spinning. He stumbled over to a chair and plopped down. As soon as he was sitting, Reggie took a tremendous leap from the workbench and landed in his lap, letting loose a croaking purr.

"Are you dizzy?" Mesmer asked. "My mechanical tutor may have been a bit harsh on you. I tried to pack in as much info as possible, but sometimes it's like trying to shove a pizza through a keyhole. You just sit tight! I can fix you right up."

"Mechanical what?" But the man was already rushing around the room, opening cabinets, over-turning crates, poking through drawers. Finally, he came up with what looked like a silver spoon. "Ah ha!" he cried.

He raced over to Eddie. "Say ahhh!" Instinctively, Eddie said *ahhh* and Mesmer slipped the 'spoon' into his mouth and pressed a button on its handle.

Instantly, it felt like a swarm of electric spiders poured into his mouth, shocking his tongue, his throat, his nose. He coughed violently, spitting the spoon across the room. The electric spiders vanished as soon as they appeared.

"Feel better?" Mesmer asked, and Eddie hated to admit that, yes, he did feel less woozy, but he sure could have done without being shocked.

"Should have warned you about the sensation. Quite shocking. Did you feel spiders or lizards? To some people they feel like lizards..."

"Spiders," Eddie whispered.

"Yes, they're the worst. Ugh! Anywhoo..."

Eddie stood up, causing Reggie to leap from his lap and skitter back to Mesmer's side. "Stop! I'm not going to listen to one more word until you answer some questions."

"Fine, fine. Go ahead."

"Who are you? Not just your name. I want to know *who you are, what a mechanical tutor is and where the heck I am!*"

Mesmer turned to him, hair flapping. Eddie got the impression that he cut it himself. And his shoes... mismatched with neon laces. "Last things first. Where do you *think* you are?"

"Well, I *was* in the abandoned house on the island."

Mesmer clapped his hands. "And that's exactly where you are, my boy."

Eddie shook his head. "But... but all of this..." he said, waving around at the makeshift laboratory.

"We're still in that abandoned house, Eddie. Both of us. We're just a little out of step with it," Mesmer said with an impish grin.

He pulled a keychain from his pocket and raised it over his head. He pressed a button, and Eddie distinctly heard the sound of a car's locking system beep.

Suddenly, Eddie found himself staring straight at Roxie, the flashlight blinding him. Roxie screamed, Eddie jumped back...

Beep! He was back in the lab with Mesmer.

"I don't understand," Eddie said.

"We are currently residing in the tiny moments in between seconds. You know how movies work? Not video but old school movies on film?"

Mesmer dashed to an old laundry cart and started rifling through a collection of old cameras and flashbulbs and pulled out a dusty movie reel. He motioned Eddie over.

"People used movie cameras to record the world frame by frame," said Mesmer, excited by his explanation. "Those frames, that's where the old house and your friends and the rest of the world live. But you see here?"

Mesmer feverishly unwound the strip of film from the reel. Eddie took the film in hand and held it up to the light. Each frame held an image just slightly different than the one before. And in between each frame was a miniscule dark space.

"This is where *we* are. In the space between frames. Hiding in plain view, just a stutter step out of synch with the rest of reality. Pretty cool, huh?"

Eddie stared at Mesmer, trying to let him know with his steely gaze that although yes, he did think it was pretty cool, he still had some unanswered questions.

"Ah, the mechanical tutor. Question two. Right," said Mesmer. He dove into yet another junk-filled crate and came up with a duplicate of the metal nut Eddie had pulled from the lake."

"That's..." Eddie said but was too shocked to go on.

"It sure is. *This* is a mechanical tutor, although that's an awfully unwieldy name, is it not? I've considered calling it a brain-nut or a think-pod, but nothing really sticks. Don't worry, I'll come up with something soon enough."

"What does it do?"

Mesmer smiled proudly. "Why, it teaches, of course. Teaches like nobody's business. I programmed it to pump ten years' worth of science and math, biology and zoology, astronomy and astrophysics into your noggin in a single zap."

Eddie's thoughts were awhirl. "Why would you do that? Why would you stick all that stuff inside my head?"

Mesmer tilted his head and considered Eddie a moment. "That's where things get a bit tricky. Do you like s'mores?"

Caught off guard, Eddie simply said, "Sure."

"Excellent!" Mesmer dashed over to an old cupboard and began pulling out ingredients. Marshmallows, chocolate bars, graham crackers. "I do love a good s'more. I find they calm me down. With all the sugar it should do quite the opposite, but it doesn't. Ah, well. It's a mystery I don't care solve."

Mesmer pulled a Bunsen burner from a pile of trash, its hose snaking behind, and lit it. He skewered a marshmallow with a bent TV antenna and set about toasting it.

"You were saying?" Eddie prompted.

"Yes, of course. Why did I shove a library's worth of data into your old noodle? An excellent question that deserves an excellent answer."

Eddie stalked over to the man, switched off the Bunsen burner and fixed his eyes on Mesmer's. "Are you going to tell me or not?"

Mesmer turned instantly serious. "I did it because it's your birthright, my boy."

"My what?"

"Your birthright. By your age, other kids like you would have had years and years of intensive study in all of the sciences. It is something that *he* denied you, something I believe it is my duty to give you back. So I built my tutor, stuffed it full of every bit of information I could and set it loose to find you. Or for you to find it. In any case..."

"You said 'he' denied me. He who?"

Mesmer swallowed. "Sly."

"Sly?"

"Vernon Sly. The maddest of them all."

With every answer, Eddie understood less and less. He gritted his teeth and said, "The maddest of who? Who are you talking about?"

Mesmer smiled wanly. He handed Eddie the s'more. "Why, your people, Eddie. The Mad Scientists of New Jersey."

CHAPTER SEVEN

Eddie took a bite of the s'more. *Crack!* It was like biting down on a rock.

"Gah! What are you trying to do, break my teeth?"

Mesmer examined the bag marshmallows. "Hmm, these seem to have expired a few years ago." He shrugged and tossed the bag into a wooden box marked *Hazardous Materials.*

Eddie plopped into a hideous orange armchair. Reggie hopped over to him, leapt once more into his lap and *rej-jipped* quietly. Eddie barely noticed.

"The Mad Scientists?" Eddie asked.

"Of New Jersey," Mesmer said pointedly. "Illinois boasted a chapter back in the day. So did Colorado. There was even a group who called themselves Mad Scientists down in Florida, but they turned out to be a bunch of quacks. Claimed to have invented a fountain of youth. Bah! Nothing but a cheap trick, all smoke and mirrors. But the community here in New Jersey, on Lake Mohawk, they were the first. And the best and the brightest."

"But... they were mad?" Eddie asked.

"That's just what they called themselves. But in truth they were only mad in the sense that they were madly creative, madly inventive, madly and passionately devoted to the art of making science."

"And I'm one of them?" Eddie's heart was pounding like a jackhammer.

"Yes. Well... no. I mean, you would have been, could have been, *should* have been. If Sly hadn't come along and ruined everything, you would be one among many young geniuses. Instead here you sit. Like the last Dodo."

What the heck is a dodo, Eddie thought, and a split second later the image of a short, squat bird popped into his head along with a swirl of information that scrolled through his mind so fast it almost gave him whiplash. A genius? Him? Forgetaboutit.

"Are you calling me a fat bird?"

Mesmer chuckled. "Of course not. You know all about the dodo, don't you? I'm sure I included it in your studies. Famed as much for its extinction as its ridiculous name. You, like that final dodo, are the last of your kind."

Eddie sat up. Reggie croaked his annoyance. "But what about you? You must be a mad scientist too. I've never met anyone more mad sciency than you."

"I suppose I do look quite the part," said Mesmer, glancing down at his attire. "I'm sorry if I must remain a bit vague on that point. But I assure you, *you* are the last."

"If I'm the last, then who was the first?" asked Eddie. "Who were these Mad Scientists?"

Mesmer grinned. "That I can tell you. Lights!" He clapped his hands. Immediately, the lights dimmed. The hum of a dozen movie projectors, video projectors and slide projectors turning on filled the room. "I give you, the lost history of the Mad Scientists of New Jersey!"

Images and filmed footage came to life, projected on every wall. Although what he was seeing was old and in black and white, Eddie recognized the lake and some of the houses next to the shore. There was Echo Island surrounded by old boats, the stately house still under construction. And there...

"Wait a minute," said Eddie, pointing at one rotating series of images. "There's no water in the lake."

He was right. The slideshow he was referring to showed Lake Mohawk without the lake. No water. None. Instead, it showed a deep valley with a small town set in the middle of it, populated by brick buildings. This one looked like a factory, that one looked like a library.

There were streets and shops and houses. All set into what was now the depths of Lake Mohawk.

"When did...?" he started to ask, but Mesmer jumped in.

"Shh! Here's the voiceover. I'm very proud of it," he whispered.

As the films, video and images continued to dance across the walls and ceiling, Mesmer's voice rang out from a score of speakers. "The year was 1920. The place: the scientific community of Voltaic Valley, home to over one hundred and fifty of the brightest minds this world has ever known."

Mesmer leaned in and whispered, "We should have popcorn for this, shouldn't we?" Eddie shook his head. Mesmer's popcorn would probably kill him. The presentation continued.

"They all gathered here, men, women and their families, to kindle the flames of scientific advancement, to pursue the secrets of the universe and to combine one and a half cups flour and three eggs to... zzz... zzz..."

Mesmer leapt up, grabbed a wrench and pounded on a glowing stereo unit. "Bit of a glitch!" *Pound!* "I'll clear it right up!" *Pound!*

The voiceover resumed. "Their goal was a simple one: to use their gifts for the betterment of mankind."

A white-haired man appeared on a number of screens dressed in old-timey clothes. Eddie recognized him at once. "That's Thomas Edison. We studied him in Mr. Hubbard's class. He invented the light bulb."

Mesmer snorted. "Among scads of other things *not* in your schoolbooks, but...shhh!"

"However, one extremely gifted member of the community found serving his fellow man to be a poor use of his skills." Images of the man popped up all around Eddie. In every photo, the man's face was either blurred or had been scratched out.

"Vernon Sly," the audio continued, "was a master mathematician and a wizard of physics. It was his contention that the people of Voltaic Valley, rather than sharing their discoveries and inventions with the rest of mankind, should toss the vegetables with butter and place them in the center of the pan... zzz... zzz..."

"Oh, come on!" Mesmer shouted as he banged away with his wrench. Reggie hopped off Eddie's lap and hid underneath a pile of boxes.

"Onions robot monkey apple zzzapple... zzzzzz!" squealed the stereo system. With one final bash, Mesmer reduced the unit to splinters. "Toothbrush... sparkplug... zzz... zzz... zzz..."

All went quiet. Panting, Mesmer clapped. The lights came back up.

"So, what happened?" asked Eddie. "What did that guy Sly do?"

Mesmer walked over to a window and stared out wistfully. "He drowned them. He drowned them all."

"He what?"

Mesmer turned back to Eddie. "Out of jealousy and spite, Vernon Sly blew up the dam holding back the Wallkill River and flooded Voltaic Valley, killing every last person in the town."

Eddie thought about this. Then that meant... "Even the kids?"

"Even himself," said Mesmer, nodding.

"Himself? That doesn't make sense. Why would he kill himself if he wanted to be such a big shot?"

"Why indeed," said Mesmer. He knelt and coaxed Reggie out from under the pile of boxes. Once he had him, he stroked the metal critter's back. Surely a robot frog wouldn't react to that, Eddie thought, but soon enough Reggie was warbling a froggy, robotic tune.

Eddie got up and started pacing the room. "But if Sly flooded the town and every last one of my mad scientist ancestors, then I shouldn't be here."

Mesmer slipped Reggie into his pocket. "Not quite. On the fateful day that Vernon Sly laid waste to Voltaic Valley, one member of the community, one single man, was absent. And you and he just so happen to share the same last name."

"You mean Thomas...?"

"That's right."

"But I'm not..."

"Yes, you are."

"Are you going to let me finish or not?" Eddie grumbled. "My dad said just because we had the same last name as a famous person, that didn't mean we were related. He said he had plenty of friends named Washington and Lincoln and *they* weren't related. To the presidents, I mean."

Mesmer walked over to Eddie and placed his hand on his shoulder. "But you *are* related. You are the great, great, great grandson of Thomas Alva Edison."

Eddie was stunned. If what Mesmer was saying was true, then his father had lied to him. But why?

A buzzer went off somewhere in the room. Just a short burst, a little *buzz*, but it set Mesmer scurrying around the room to locate its source. "I have so many bells, buzzers and alarms hooked up to so many things I can't quite keep all of them straight. Perhaps I have something in one of the ovens." He stepped over to a tower of microwave ovens and opened each door in succession. "Nope, nope and... nope."

Eddie wanted to go home. Maybe coming here was a bad idea. He would have handled it better if Dad were with him. Or even Roxie and Pudge. They must be wondering where he was. Would they leave without him? If they did, what would he do? Swim back home?

"You know, I think it's time for me to go."

"But you just got here." Mesmer seemed deflated. "We have *so* much to talk about."

"Yeah, I think I'm all talked out for tonight. If you'll just press that little clicker device or whatever it is, I'll be heading back." Eddie started backing toward the door.

"Wait!" Mesmer shouted, racing over to a closet and throwing wide the door. An avalanche of junk poured out and Mesmer dug through it wildly.

Eddie took advantage of the man's distraction to race to the front door. Just as his hand touched the knob, a buzzer went off again, only this time it didn't stop short. *Buzz, buzz, buzz!* A red light above the door burst to life, flashing in rhythm with the sound.

Mesmer bolted out of the closet and stared up at the blinking light. He had something in his hands. Was that a tool belt?

"Here!" Mesmer cried and tossed the thing to Eddie. Eddie caught it. No, not a tool belt. It looked more like a superhero's utility belt – leather with five metal bars the size of chewing gum packs stitched in at regular intervals. "Put it on!"

"What is it?"

"You're going to have to figure that out for yourself," said Mesmer.

Eddie was peeved. "And why is that?"

Mesmer stared up at the pulsing red light. "Because I just remembered what that buzzer is for."

Something slammed against the door. Eddie stepped back as a shrill whistle pierced the night. Whatever was outside struck the door again, sending cracks zigzagging up and down, left and right.

Eddie darted back to where Mesmer stood frozen. "How did it find us?" Mesmer gasped. "How could it possibly navigate to this in-between time?"

"I don't know what it is, but it's going to get inside very, *very* soon!" shouted Eddie.

"Put on the belt!" Mesmer screamed, and Eddie did as he was told, covering it with his shirt. The thing outside let loose with another nightmare whistle.

Mesmer turned Eddie to face him. "You asked me why Vernon Sly drowned himself along with the others. I think he did it because he knew that somehow he could come back."

"Come back? How?"

The wooden door shattered, splinters of wood exploding into the room. Eddie caught his breath as the thing stepped through the ruined doorway.

Its eyes were bright red, like stoplights. It had a long metallic neck and a barrel-like body. It stomped the ground with massive, hooved feet. Sprouting from its back were a pair of shiny, metal wings. If the thing had been flesh and blood rather than steel, Eddie could have sworn he was staring into the eyes of the Jersey Devil.

The metal beast belched steam and whistled its earsplitting whistle.

"I'll catch up with you once you figure out the belt," cried Mesmer. "In the meantime, take care of Reggie, will you?" The man pulled the mechanical frog from his pocket and thrust it into Eddie's arms. Mesmer pulled his keychain from his pocket and raised it into the air as the creature charged straight for them, clanking as it came.

"He needs a little oil at night!" Mesmer shouted and pressed the button.

The lumbering metal beast reached out toward Eddie and he squeezed his eyes shut tight. There was a *crack* and a flash of light so bright that Eddie could see it through his eyelids. And then...

Everything went silent. There was no sound but the chirp of crickets. Eddie opened his eyes. He was back in the abandoned version of the house. Mesmer, the mechanical monster – had they been real at all?

"*Rej-jip!*" He looked down. There, still clutched in his hands, was Reggie staring up at him with his little yellow eyes.

"Don't worry, little guy. I think we're safe."

A white light pierced the darkness, hitting Eddie square in the face. He put a hand to his face to shield his eyes. The devil, the machine, whatever it was had followed him!

A laugh echoed in the darkness – a cruel, familiar laugh. Eddie squinted and saw a figure step forward and lower the flashlight.

"Safe?" Lance hissed. "Oh, you're a long way from being safe, munch."

CHAPTER EIGHT

It was almost three in the morning when Eddie and his mother got back home. Cooper, who had been fast asleep on the sofa, trotted over to nuzzle him with his wet nose and then put himself to bed in his crate.

Eddie got the silent treatment from his mom on the ride back, but not so now. She was furious.

"Imagine getting a call from the police in the middle of the night," she said, clenching her hands.

And that's exactly what had happened. Apparently Eddie and his friends weren't the only ones who had decided to sneak out that night. Lance was hanging out with a girl on his boat when he spied the flashlight shining about on Echo Island. When he went over to investigate, he found Pudge asleep on *The Cheesy Breezy* and Roxie hunting around, trying to find Eddie.

Lance called in backup. Soon, Hedges and Babcock were steering their way toward the island as well. The three of them searched every inch of Echo Island and could not find Eddie. Suddenly a flash of lightning lit up the night, and Lance caught Eddie in his flashlight beam.

Rather than issuing Eddie and company a reprimand, Lance called the police. He and the rest of the Mustache Mafia took Eddie, Roxie and Pudge straight to the boardwalk where two police cruisers were waiting for them.

"Smell you later," scoffed Lance as he handed Eddie over to the officer. Eddie sat petrified in the back seat as he watched officers usher Roxie and Pudge into the back of their own cars. Pudge tossed him a glance that told him what he already knew: they were in deep doo-doo.

The back seat smelled horrible, and Eddie gagged. "Sorry," said the officer behind the wheel. "Had a guy lose his lunch back there. I'll crack the window." He did, but just a crack.

After waiting at the police station for over an hour, Eddie's mother had arrived, still in her pajamas. Her eyes were red, and Eddie instantly regretted the night's excursion. His mother had been through enough already with his father's disappearance, having to keep their sagging roof over their head all by herself. He felt awful.

The sergeant on duty had taken Reggie from him when he first arrived, more out of curiosity than anything, but as Eddie and his mother were leaving, the man had given back the metal frog.

"My niece would love one of these. Where did you get it?"

"I'm just holding onto it for a friend," said Eddie. Which was only half true. He was just holding onto Reggie for the time being, but could he count Mesmer as a friend? He had grave doubts about that.

Now, he sat stroking Reggie's metal back as his mother paced about his cluttered bedroom. The frog seemed to know better than to sing.

"Do you have anything to say for yourself?" Eddie's mother asked.

"Sorry," Eddie said, but it wasn't an answer, simply a plea for his mother to drop it and let him go to bed and forget about the whole night.

But she didn't drop it. She didn't ground Eddie right then and there. Instead she said he'd have to think about what the consequences were, which was even worse.

Before he went to sleep, Eddie stripped off the leather belt Mesmer had insisted he take and examined it. It wasn't all that remarkable. Just a leather strap with those five metal packs attached.

Eddie slept fitfully. His dreams were filled with monsters. The next morning, his mother woke him before his alarm went off. "Get up. We have a meeting with your principal." She was *not* happy.

Eddie almost shook as he sat across from Mr. Wood in his office, his mother seething next to him. Principal Wood was a beefy man with a short, military haircut. He never blinked. He ticked off a list of Eddie's misdeeds: breaking school property (the intercom), destroying a teacher's property (Mr. Hubbard's toupee) and impersonating a school lunch aide.

He had also received a phone call from the police informing him of Eddie, Roxie and Pudge's late night escapades.

"We have a regular process to deal with these sorts of things, Mrs. Edison. But seeing as this is the first time Eddie has ever acted up, I suggest you take him out of school for the next couple of days for a family vacation."

Eddie's mother looked puzzled. "I can't. I have a business trip I need to take this week. I landed the voiceover for a new app. The Testy Taster, they call it. For people who want to complain about restaurants. They want me to record it in the city. New York, I mean." It seemed Mr. Wood made everyone nervous.

The principal smiled. "I use the word vacation very loosely. It could mean a trip to sunny Florida, I love going down to the Keys, myself. Or it could mean a visit to one's own home. Without television or computer privileges."

"I'm not sure I understand."

The principal leaned in to his mother. "If we go the suspension route, that goes in Eddie's record. Let's save that for the next time." He looked to Eddie. "Even though there won't be a next time, will there?" Eddie shook his head vigorously.

So it was that Eddie found himself under house arrest, or so he saw it. He was not to watch his shows or play his games or doing anything at all but work through a list of chores his mother was leaving for him. When she insisted he use his phone for emergency calls only, Eddie had to confess that he had broken it, which only made his mother even more upset.

She rooted around in the kitchen drawers until she found her old phone and gave it to him. "I'll be back on Saturday," she said as she rolled her suitcase to the front door. "Don't give Martha any trouble. And remember: 911 calls *only*."

And like that, his mother was off, and he was alone with his parents' family friend Martha and her cranky old husband Abel.

"Don't worry, Eddie," said Martha with a wink as she pulled a bag of candy from her purse and held it out to him. "Your father pulled worse stunts than you, believe me."

"You were there, weren't you?" asked Eddie, waving off the candy. "The night he disappeared? That night at the diner?"

Martha's face closed and she turned away. Abel simply grunted, plopped himself down on the sofa and proceeded to fall fast asleep.

***

Chore number fourteen on Eddie's list was vacuuming. He pulled out the family's old Hoover and checked the bag while Cooper made a mad dash for the basement. Cooper was a brave dog, always ready to bark a stranger away from his yard, but when it came to the vacuum, he was terrified.

Eddie got down to the boring business of vacuuming the living room, the hallways, the den. Old Abel grumbled even more when Eddie had to clean under the sofa he was snoozing on. Martha didn't seem to mind, though. She was busy making lunch in the kitchen.

As soon as Eddie turned the vacuum off, he heard Cooper barking his head off in the basement. Had he cornered a mouse? The little critters had been known to pop through the air vents in Mom's booth, causing her to shriek in the middle of recording.

Eddie went to the kitchen and grabbed a broom.

"I hope you like egg salad," Martha said.

"I sure do," Eddie lied. In fact, he hated the stuff. To him, it tasted like craft paste gone bad. "I'll be back up in a minute." He headed down the stairs.

Cooper was still barking. "Cool it, Coop," Eddie called. The dog definitely had something backed into a corner next to his father's workbench and was very eager to get at it. Eddie nudged him aside and raised the broom over his head.

A small, trembling voice came from the shadows. *"Rej-jip? Rej-jip, rej- jip?"*

"Reggie, how did you get out?" Eddie lowered his broom and knelt. He had left the frog in his desk drawer, but apparently Reggie was an escape artist. He held out his hand, and Reggie took two tentative hops forward, saw Cooper and scurried back into the corner.

Eddie picked up the metal frog and set him on the workbench which was littered with spools of solder, vacuum tubes, home appliances his father had always meant to fix but had never gotten around to.

The frog wiggled happily, nestled into a pile of old clock parts. Maybe he thinks he's back home with Mesmer, Eddie thought.

He looked around the room. Mom's audio booth sat up against the cinderblock wall. It was a big, black box about the size of a large refrigerator. Inside was a microphone, recording equipment and, as he had learned the one time he had peeked inside, a framed photo of his mom and dad when they were young and happy. Before he came along. Before Dad went missing.

A sneeze at the top of the stairs caused Cooper's ears to go on alert, but his tail was soon wagging as old Abel appeared, coming down the steps slowly, wiping his nose with his handkerchief.

"I gotta use the can," the old man said as he reached the bottom of the stairs.

"The bathroom's upstairs, Mr. Sparks," Eddie said, but Abel kept on coming toward him. "Really, it's upstairs past my bedroom. You can't miss it."

Reggie chose that moment to let loose his loudest *rej-jip* yet. It echoed through the basement like a car horn. Abel's eyes fixed on the frog. "What in tarnation have you got there?"

Eddie instinctively stepped in front of Reggie. Mr. Sparks couldn't tell the difference between a basement and a bathroom. Who knew what he would do to the frog if he got his hands on it?

"Nothing!" Eddie said quickly. "Hey, I thought I heard Mrs. Sparks calling us. I think lunch must be ready."

Abel curled his lip. "Egg salad sandwiches. The woman knows I despise egg salad." Eddie smiled at this – it was nice to know that he wasn't the only one who hated the stuff. In that moment of distraction, the old man grabbed Reggie off the workbench.

"*Rej-JIP!*" Reggie cried.

"What do you got sending current to this thing's vocal cells, a bridge rectifier? No wonder its voice is fried." Abel flipped the twitching, complaining Reggie over on his back, grabbed a pair of metal shears and slit him up the stomach like a fisherman gutting a trout.

"Stop!" Eddie wailed.

"Oh, quit your crying. If you had done this right the first time, I wouldn't have to go in and clean up your mess. You're just like your father."

At the mention of his father, Eddie's attention turned from the squirming frog to the old man. "You used to do stuff like this with my dad?"

"Of course I did," said Abel. "How else was he going to learn? It's not like he had anyone else to teach him. Not like in the old days."

"What old days?" Eddie coaxed.

"Hand me the needle-nose pliers," Abel barked. "The old days. Back when folks actually knew how to invent, gosh darn it. All gone, all gone now. Only thing left is their junk, leftovers for the rest of us to poke through and wonder about. No, I said the *needle-nose* pliers!"

It was the most lucid Eddie had ever seen Mr. Sparks. Usually he slipped in and out, like a radio station that came and went. But right now? The way the old guy's hands were flying around the workbench, collecting bits of wire, diodes, paperclips, he seemed almost young again.

"Only a matter of time before this little fella's brainpan was scrambled. Who taught you how to lay down circuits?"

"No one," Eddie replied, but almost instantly he knew that wasn't the truth. As fast as Abel was moving, Eddie was actually *following* what he was doing, *understanding* every step. Mesmer had taught him. Mesmer and his nutty tutor. The Nutty Tutor... that was a pretty good name. He'd have to remember to share it with Mesmer if he ever saw him again.

"Change the polarity of this micro-speaker, attach an input line and..." The old man sealed the metal frog's belly back up with a line of solder, leaving a single wire trailing out from its neck. He stripped the end of the wire bare and slipped it into the side of his mouth.

"Say ribbit," growled Mr. Sparks.

"*Griggy!*" croaked Reggie.

Abel gave the frog a shake. "Say ribbit."

"*Turp-chock!*"

The old man grumbled, grabbed a screwdriver and made a small adjustment.

"Now, say ribbit!"

Reggie's eye lights blinked twice, then he said, "*Now, say ribbit!*"

"No!"

"*Say ribbit, say ribbit, say ribbit,*" the happy mechanical creature chirped.

"Forget it. Return to default," he ordered.

"*Rej-jip,*" Reggie yipped.

Abel tossed the frog to Eddie, yanking out the wire umbilical. "Best I can do."

"How did you get him to change what he says?" Eddie asked.

"You were right here watching, weren't you? I just set up a neural link, a phone call from my brain to his. But next time, start with the right parts. I swear I spied some telegraph line holding the relays in place. Garbage in, garbage out. Next time you start a project, take it one step at a time, Bill. Don't rush. One step at a time."

"Bill was my father, Mr. Sparks," Eddie said.

The old man's gruff demeanor crumbled before Eddie's eyes. "I gotta use the can," he mumbled.

"It's upstairs. Here, lemme show you." Eddie led the old man to the stairs. "Play nice," he called back to Cooper, who was again eyeing Reggie with territorial disdain. "I'll be back."

***

While forcing down the dreaded egg salad, something the old man had said kept looping through his brain. "Take it one step at a time."

After excusing himself, Eddie went to his bedroom, retrieved the leather belt and headed back down to the basement. To his disbelief, he found Reggie perched on Cooper's back. The mechanical frog's front legs were vibrating rapidly, giving the dog a vigorous back massage. Apparently the two had settled their differences. Cooper was in heaven.

"I don't even wanna ask," Eddie said, shaking his head.

He unrolled the belt on the workbench. What was it? What did it do? And why was Mesmer so keen to give it to him? The odd man had told him he'd have to figure it out on his own, but why? So many questions, so few answers.

Take it one step at a time. First, he examined the belt itself. He had initially thought the strap was made up of a single piece of leather, but when he looked closer, he saw that it was actually two pieces stitched together. He also noticed that there was something stitched up inside.

He ran the length of the belt between his fingers. He could feel hidden wires running from one of the packs to the next. He looked at the packs. They were made of a tough plastic, like something an old radio might be made of. The word *Bakelite* flashed into his head along with the knowledge that yes, the packs were indeed made of this antique material.

Set in the top of each of the packs was a small lens not unlike the lens of a flashlight.

And that was it.

"Next step," he said to himself as he cinched the belt around his waist. He stood there wondering what to do next. The first thing that came to mind was that it looked like a superhero's utility belt – something Captain Panda or Dr. Mosquito from TV would wear.

Eddie bent his knees. "Up we go!" he shouted and leapt into the air.

He only made it about four inches off the ground. "Well, it was worth a try," he said to Cooper, who had fallen asleep while Reggie scratched his ears.

Maybe it was some sort of protective gear. Maybe it created a force field that would block bullets, rockets, whatever anyone might throw at him.

Eddie picked up a heavy roll of duct tape and tossed it in the air. "Force field on!" It hit him in the head with a *thunk* and he winced.

Then he burped – a long, liquid belch. *Ugh! Egg salad! Disgusting!* He needed to clear his mouth. His mom kept a mini fridge next to her booth filled with water and juice to keep her going while she was working. He threw open the door. Empty.

The overpowering taste of slimy egg and mustard filled his mouth. How could people eat the stuff? And on purpose? He wished he had a slice of Pudge's father's pizza. *Mmm.* Piled high with cheese, the sauce still scalding hot from the oven, the crust...

A light turned on behind one of the lenses in one of the packs on the belt. It shone pale orange. What in the world?

Eddie watched the light as it stuttered, flickered and then went out. What had turned it on, he wondered? Surely it wasn't his eggy burp? That would be more likely to kill a mad sciency device than bring it to life.

What had he been doing when it turned on? He'd been thinking about the pizza, thinking about the cheese and the sauce and the...

The light clicked back on.

It was something about the pizza. What was so special about the pizza. Well, what wasn't special about it? It *was* the best pizza he'd ever had. The only thing that had gotten in the way of his enjoying that slice completely had been the oddly sweet scent of pine air freshener that Roxie used in place of perfume.

A second light turned on. Pale green.

Memories! This belt was picking up on his memories. And not just any memories, one specific memory.

He closed his eyes and replayed that day in Pop's Pizzeria through his head. He had been sitting with Pudge and Roxie while Pop had been serving the pizza. He remembered that Pop had a smear of pizza sauce right across his apron.

A blue light clicked on. *Sight.* The image of that sauce stain. How many senses were there? Eddie tried to think but his mind was racing. Taste: check. Smell: check. Sight: check. What else, what else?

Touch.

A vivid memory of Roxie bumping against him, sending tingles down his arm set off the next pack. Purple.

There was one more, he knew it. Five senses, five packs. What would happen when light number five went off?

Cooper woke up just then to find Reggie scratching his belly. The dog jumped up and started barking at the frog, but now in a friendly way. The two new pals started barking and croaking and yapping and yipping in circles around Eddie.

"Be quiet, you two! I can't hear myself think!"

That was it. *Sound.*

The phones. The phones at Pop's were ringing off the hook because it was the start of the dinner rush.

The fifth light turned on. Yellow.

His whole body started to vibrate. The room began to spin. Either that or Eddie's brain did. Whichever was true, he was about to lose his lunch.

Just as his gorge began to rise there was a *bang*. The basement was gone. Instead, he found himself in the booth of Pop's Pizzeria sitting across from Roxie in her ratty sweater, her mouth agape.

He was also sitting across from himself.

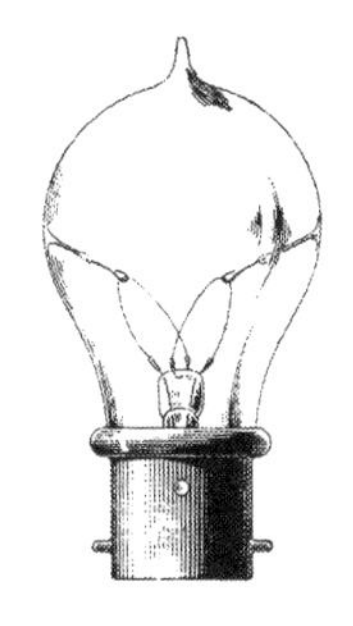

CHAPTER NINE

Roxie squeaked. His other self stared in slack-jawed disbelief. Eddie was certain that the look on his own face was a mirror image.

"Who...?" the other Eddie asked.

Roxie picked up a plastic fork and wielded it like a weapon. "What are you? A clone? A robot? An evil twin?"

Eddie shook his head. "I'm just me. Eddie."

Other Eddie glared at him. "What are you doing with my face?"

"I could ask you the same thing," Eddie countered.

Eddie looked toward the kitchen. Pudge was busy answering the phone for his father who was even busier spreading mozzarella over half a dozen pizzas.

This was yesterday just after the incident with the black hole and the toupee and... and... Eddie could hardly believe it. The belt! Somehow, it had sent him back in time.

Roxie pinched his arm. "Ouch!" he squealed. "Why'd you do that?"

Roxie turned to the other Eddie. "He feels real."

"That's because I *am* real," Eddie said. He caught his other self burning holes in him with his eyes. "I'm you. I'm just one day older, that's all. I've traveled twenty-some hours back in time."

"Why?" the other Eddie asked.

"Huh?"

Other Eddie shook his head. "If you're me and you've managed to travel across time and space..."

"Not space, just time," Eddie said.

"Whatever!" the other Eddie fumed. "If, by some miracle, you've come here from the future, then you must have a pretty big reason for doing so."

Eddie gulped. A reason? Nope. He'd managed it mostly by accident. Now that he thought about it, he had no clue how he was going to get back. Was he doomed to forever be a day behind in a world where another version of himself would be forever throwing him nasty looks?

Eddie felt a buzzing at his waist and looked down at the belt. The orange light was blinking. Now, the red was blinking too. His whole body vibrated again. If that tingling sensation was any indication, this was going to be a very short trip.

"Well?" the other Eddie pressed.

"I came back because... because..." He reached out, grabbed the slice of pizza out of other Eddie's hand. "Because I hate egg salad sandwiches!"

And *bang!* He was back in his basement as if nothing had happened. Cooper looked up at him, annoyed at being awakened. Reggie *rej-jipped* a hello.

"Thank goodness I didn't fly right by the present and go shooting off into the future," Eddie thought.

He looked down. He still had the slice of cheese pizza gripped in his hand. Famished, Eddie wolfed down the slice, tossing the crust to a grateful Cooper.

Eddie suddenly realized what a missed opportunity his trip to the past had been. Of course! He had traveled back to the time before he and his friends had taken their midnight cruise, before they had landed on the island. Before he had met Mesmer. If he were to go back to the pizza parlor, he could warn himself not to visit the island. He could avoid meeting that crazy scientist and then maybe, just maybe, his life would go back to normal.

But do you really want that?

The thought surprised him. What surprised him even more was the answer. *No.* Going back to normal would mean giving something up, something Mesmer had told him that fellow Sly had stolen from him.

My birthright. He was the last of a long line of Mad Scientists, and even though his brain struggled to convince him otherwise, he knew it was true.

Reggie's head suddenly spun completely around. Once, twice. His yellow eyes flashed, he opened his mouth and an old fashioned telephone ring echoed from his throat. This was too much for Cooper, who got up and quickly disappeared upstairs.

Eddie picked the metal frog up, shook him and said, "Hello?"

"Hellooo!" came Mesmer's voice from Reggie's mouth, though he sounded tinny and distant. "Can you hear me? Hellooo?"

"I can hear you, I can hear you." Eddie wondered if talking to Mesmer was a violation of his mother's insistence that he only use the phone for emergencies. But his wasn't a phone – it was a frog. Besides, he'd consider jumping back and forth in time an emergency any day. "How are you calling me?"

"Oh, Reggie's full of tricks and surprises. He's also full of a mad dose of technology. Did I mention that I programed him to be able to sing every last one of Mozart's operas? Would you like to hear..."

"No!" said Eddie. "What I would like are some answers."

There was some static on the line, and Reggie wriggled in his hands. Then Mesmer's voice was back, clearer this time. "I'm back, I'm back. Looks like I've got to bump his bandwidth. Anywho, I see that you've already made your first jump. Good for you! I knew you'd figure it out. Eventually."

"How do you know I... jumped?"

"Oh, I have my ways," Mesmer said, mysteriously. "You left a little ripple when you went – a little eddy in the waters of time. Ha! You made an eddy, Eddie!"

Eddie groaned. Was it even worth trying to get any answers out of the man? "How can a person travel through time? It doesn't make any sense!"

"*Sense* is exactly right, as you no doubt discovered. The belt keys into a moment in the past, into a moment in *your* past, directed by your five senses."

"My past? But what if I wanted to travel back to the Wild West or to ancient Greece?" Eddie asked.

"You can't," the voice inside the frog's mouth said. "The device you're wearing can only take you to your own timeline. If you weren't there to smell, taste, see, touch or hear it, you're out of luck."

Reggie's head spun around once and the static returned. Mesmer was still talking, but his voice sounded wobbly and distorted. "You're breaking up and I still have questions!" Eddie called down the frog's throat. "I want to know what that thing was that broke down your door! I want to know...!"

"*Crackle-crackle...* meet... *crackle...* bring your friends... *zzz...* I'll... *zzzt- crackle...* answers. Four o'clock at... *crrrr...* bowling alley. And don't forget to..."

The line went dead. Reggie woke as if from a daze. "Rej...?" Eddie set him back down on the cluttered workbench.

Four o'clock. Bowling alley. Friends. It must be about two now. Apparently, Mesmer wanted to meet him at the bowling alley with Roxie and Pudge. But why? So they could form a bowling league?

And just how was he supposed to get in touch with them with his mother's ban on personal phone calls looming over him?

"Instead of calling, why don't I slip back in time and tell them to meet me at the bowling alley at four?" he thought. "It couldn't hurt to practice this time traveling stuff."

He started thinking about pizza again, then stopped. He didn't have to go back as far as their after school visit to the pizzeria. No, he needed to zip back to the last time that he, Roxie and Pudge had all been together. When exactly was that?

The last time he saw Pudge, he was getting into the back of the police cruiser. Pudge was trying not to cry, and Roxie was pouting angrily.

Eddie kicked his memory into overdrive. He heard the crackle of the police scanner. "10-9, officers on scene." He saw the flashing red and blue lights. He smelled the funky scent of the backseat of the cruiser, felt the breeze as the officer behind the wheel cracked the window. He tasted... what?

Darn! He looked down. Only four of the five packs on the belt were lit. Taste. He couldn't remember. How did he hope to manage the trip back?

Eddie suddenly recalled a metallic taste that had filled his mouth. He had been so nervous and afraid. The taste must have been the result of all that adrenaline coursing through his system.

Bang!

The shift was instantaneous this time. No gradual twirling into the past. He was shot directly into the backseat of that cruiser.

Of course, he materialized right next to the other Eddie. "You again!" his twin cried.

Eddie had no time for conversation. He leaned over to the barely open window and shouted, "Roxie! Pudge! Lake Mohawk Lanes, four o'clock tomorrow! Four o'clock tomorrow…!"

Crack! He was back in the basement.

He caught a whiff of smoke and looked down at the belt to see all the lights flickering on and off. It started to get warm around his waist. He unbuckled it and let it fall to the ground. The belt gave a small *zz-zzt!* and was still. Thank goodness. With Eddie's luck, he could imagine it bursting into flames.

Two hours. He had two hours before he had to meet Mesmer. Then he'd see if his little trick in the police cruiser had paid off. He'd need to sneak out without his 'babysitters' noticing. Getting one over on Abel would be a breeze, but Martha would be another matter.

A smile spread across his lips as a plan leapt to mind. He looked over at Reggie. Maybe having a head full of new information wasn't such a bad thing after all.

***

It was around three-thirty when Martha came by Eddie's bedroom with a plate of carrot sticks and cheese. She stopped at the closed door and knocked. She knew boys his age prized their privacy.

"Eddie, I've got a snack for you," she cooed.

"I don't feel so good. I think I'll take a nap," the voice on the other side of the door croaked.

Martha didn't like the sound of that. She hoped the boy hadn't picked up Abel's cold. "Are you sure?"

"I don't feel so good," the voice repeated.

"All right," Martha said. "I'll check back on you around dinnertime."

"I think I'll take a nap,"

"That's fine, Eddie." Martha turned and headed back down the hall, munching on a carrot stick. Had the sound of the crunch not been so loud inside her head, she might have heard the voice on the other side of the door say, "*Rej- jip!*"

***

Eddie figured that if he could get to the bowling alley and back before six, he had a good chance of not being missed. Reconfiguring Reggie to respond to anyone who came to his bedroom door had been easy. He'd just repeated the steps he'd seen Abel take when he was trying to get Reggie to say *ribbit.*

He steered his bike down Mulberry Street, pedaling up one hill, zipping down the next. There were a few boats out on the lake, but nothing like the number that would be there in a few weeks when the summer season kicked in. Usually at this time of year his mind would be on boating and camping and hanging out with Pudge, but now his head was swimming with thoughts of brain-zapping nuts and time travel belts and crazy scientists.

He passed the main Lake Mohawk plaza with its gift shops and restaurants. People milled about on the wooden boardwalk overlooking the lake without a care in the world. Wouldn't that be nice, Eddie thought.

He negotiated traffic as he reached the busier main street into town. He spied the neon sign for Lake Mohawk Lanes. A smaller sign below boasted, "*Fun for all ages.*"

As Eddie approached the building, he noticed two things. First, he saw Roxie's old bike chained to the bike rack. Good, at least she had gotten his message. The second thing he saw was a purple, convertible sports car boasting a vanity license plate.

LANCE ONE

Oh, boy. Why had Mesmer chosen the bowling alley for their meeting? He knew what he'd find the minute he stepped foot inside – Lance and the rest of the Mustache Mafia sitting at lane number seven, their regular spot, making fun of the other bowlers.

He parked his bike next to Roxie's and lifted his shirt to adjust the belt. At least it had stopped smoking, but it was still warm to the touch.

Eddie looked up at the bowling alley doors. Here goes nothing, he said to himself.

The place was packed. It was Twofer Day which meant that you got two games for the price of one. Usually Mrs. Branch, the owner of the alley, was such a cheapskate, but the success of Twofer Day looked like it was something she could get behind.

Eddie scanned the place. He caught sight of Roxie's shock of red hair over at lane five. Pudge sat next to her eating an overpriced hotdog.

Just beyond them lounged Lance and his crew. Eddie gulped, put his head down and started to make his way to his friends.

"No street shoes!" a harsh voice called out. Eddie turned to see Mrs. Branch glaring at him.

"Sorry," Eddie said. After handing over both his sneakers and some cash, he made his way toward his friends in the most uncomfortable pair of bowling shoes he had ever worn.

Before any of the Mustache Mafia could catch a glimpse of him, Eddie planted himself in a seat next to Roxie with his back to lane seven.

"They let you out on good behavior?" Pudge asked as he polished off the last of his hotdog.

Eddie rubbed his feet. "I snuck out. How you guys doing?"

"I've got to work forty extra hours for my dad," said Pudge. "They like him down at the police station. He's always donating pies for fundraising events and stuff. But he is *not* happy with me."

Eddie looked to Roxie. "And you?" he asked.

Roxie was staring down at her feet. "I hate that Mrs. Branch. She tried to make me pay double because I wear two different sized bowling shoes. I threatened to post about it and she backed off."

A howl of laughter went up from the Mustache Mafia as Hedges hit a passing kid with a dollop of mustard. It was Jimmy Ticks. The kid looked over to where Eddie and the others sat, hopeful that they'd wave him over. Pudge shook his head. Jimmy got the clue and headed off to find some napkins to remove the offending mustard.

"Did you have to sit so close to those guys?" Eddie asked.

Pudge threw up his hands. "There weren't any other lanes. Why'd you call us here, anyway?" He paused. "Hold that thought." He let loose with a tremendous burp. "I ate too fast. I gotta get a soda. You want anything?"

Eddie and Roxie shook their heads. "More for me," Pudge said. "Be right back." And off he went toward the snack bar.

Roxie leaned in. "I don't think he knows what you did." Eddie let her continue. "He was busy on the phone at the pizzeria when you popped by. And I'm pretty sure he didn't see that there were two of you in the back of that cruiser. Do you think he should know that you've learned to bop in and out of time, or do you want to keep that between us?"

Eddie had no desire to keep Pudge in the dark. About anything. He was his best friend, after all, but if he brought it up now, he'd have a lot of explaining to do. Not like with Roxie. She seemed to take the whole idea rather calmly.

"Let's keep it to ourselves. For now," he said.

"You going to tell me how you managed that little trick?" she asked.

He lifted his shirt to show her the belt when Pudge approached. "I got you both a hotdog anyway. They're two-for-one, too."

Eddie was about to tell his friend that he wasn't hungry when a snide voice echoed behind him, "Oh, waiter! Are those my hotdogs?" It was Lance. Eddie could hear Babcock and Hedges snickering.

Pudge nodded at Lance, laughing silently as if he appreciated the joke, but he didn't respond. He sat down, setting the plate of hotdogs on the scoring table. "So, what's the story, Edison?"

Eddie looked to Roxie. "Well, like I was telling her..." Eddie stumbled - he was terrible at lying. Whenever he tried, he got incredibly tongue-tied. "Like I was... I mean..."

Pudge raised his eyebrows. Eddie wasn't the only one who knew he couldn't lie to save his life. "You were saying?"

A hand clapped down on Eddie's shoulder. "What's the holdup, waiter?" Lance was breathing down his neck as he stared maliciously at Pudge. "Bring those dogs over."

Eddie looked up into Lance's face. Lance looked down at him, and a dawning recognition spread across his face. "If it isn't the midnight cruisers. Have a fun time with the police last night?"

Eddie shrugged Lance's hand from his shoulder. "We're busy."

Lance shook his head. "Oh yeah?" He turned to Babcock and Hedges. "You know, if my old man caught me out on a boat in the middle of the night, he'd ground me for a month."

"Mine would ground me for a year," Hedges added with a snort.

"No, he wouldn't," Babcock said and elbowed Hedges in the ribs.

"I'll bet none of your parents know you're out. And I'll also bet that if I called them, they'd hit the roof." Lance pulled out his phone. "Let's start with you, chubs. I've got Pop's Pizzeria in my contacts."

Pudge stood and held out the hotdogs. "Here. Now, leave us alone."

Lance's wispy mustache twitched. He stepped around Eddie and whapped the plate of dogs out of Pudge's hand. "Don't tell me what to do."

Roxie stood as well. She looked down at Eddie, nodding for him to do the same. He rose, reluctantly and both he and Roxie stepped to Pudge's side. Instantly, Hedge and Babcock were out of their seats and flanking Lance.

"Hey, boys," Lance said to his cronies as he cracked his knuckles. "I got fat boy."

Just as Lance reached out and grabbed Pudge's shirt, all of the screens above the lanes went dark, wiping out the scores of every game. A collective cry went up from the bowlers. "Where's my score?" "Turn it back on!" "We're not done yet!"

Suddenly, a man sporting crazed hair and a mischievous smile appeared on every screen. It was Mesmer!

"Helloooo bowlers!" he said. "Happy Twofer Day. For the next five minutes, and five minutes only, any bowler getting three strikes in a row (not one, not two but three) will receive a three-month free pass to Lake Mohawk Lanes! Starting... now!"

A wounded shriek echoed from Mrs. Branch's office. She stuck her head out and barked, "That's not true! Who said that?" But she was drowned out by a sea of cheering kids.

Babcock and Hedges ducked away from Lance's side and shoved each other aside, each trying to get to his bowling ball first.

"What do you think you're doing?" Lance shouted at them.

"Three months," Babcock whined. "Free!"

Lance looked down the line of alleys. Everyone was frantically going for their strikes. He let go of Pudge's shirt. "I'll be right back." He turned, grabbed his bowling ball and muscled in front of Babcock and Hedges.

Eddie hadn't realized he'd been holding his breath. He exhaled and sat. He turned to find Mesmer sitting right next to him dressed in the ugliest bowling shirt he had ever seen. Mesmer smiled.

"So, where's the belt?"

CHAPTER TEN

The bowling alley had gone suddenly quiet. Eddie glanced around. There wasn't a bowler in sight. Other than Mesmer in his lime-green bowling shirt.

Eddie noticed that even Roxie and Pudge had vanished. He was miffed. "You used your clicker, didn't you? To shift us out of sync."

Mesmer rose and began examining his choice in bowling balls. "Makes it easier to talk, doesn't it?"

"What about my friends?"

"What about them?" Mesmer asked.

"You told me to bring them."

"I most certainly did not," Mesmer insisted. "Why would I want them tagging along? We have business to attend to, you and I."

"But you..." Eddie closed his mouth. The frog-phone call *had* ended in a lot of static. Perhaps instead of asking him to bring Pudge and Roxie along, Mesmer had asked him to leave them behind.

No matter. "I don't care. I want them here."

"Even the boy?"

"His name is Pudge."

Mesmer stifled a laugh. "Exceedingly odd name. Are you sure? I heard you debating whether or not to tell him about your trips through time. Like you were protecting him."

Eddie thought about this. Maybe he was trying to protect Pudge. Why was that? Roxie had figured out that he was stepping in and out of time rather quickly, and it didn't bother him one bit that she knew. He actually found it comforting to have someone know his little secret.

But Pudge? Maybe it was because Roxie was a new friend, and he'd known Pudge since they were in nursery school together. And maybe he didn't want their friendship to change. Once he knew just *how* different Eddie's life had become, Pudge might be jealous or feel awkward around him. Eddie could count the friends he had on one hand. Actually, on two fingers. And one of those was Pudge.

Still, if he was going to move further into this mystery, he'd want Pudge at his side.

"Just do it," he said.

Mesmer shrugged and produced the clicker from his pocket. There was a slight flash, and then Roxie and Pudge popped out of thin air.

"Whuh?" stammered Pudge, his eyes going wide.

Roxie seemed ticked off. "I didn't give anyone permission to yank me through time. Where am I? In the future or the past?"

"Neither," piped up Mesmer as he found the right bowling ball, walked with it to the lane and sent it spinning toward the pins.

Eddie tried to explain. "You didn't go backward or forward. You kind of went sideways."

"Whuh?" Pudge repeated. He still couldn't get over the disappearance of a bowling alley's worth of kids.

"We're in between frames," Eddie explained, pointing up at the scorecard on the screen. "It's like we're in between frame one and frame two. Right?" He looked to Mesmer who was frowning at the single pin he had knocked down.

"Yes, yes," Mesmer said sounding impatient. "In between seconds, in between frames. We've been through all that already."

Roxie threw him a hard look. "Not with me, you haven't." She walked toward the wild-haired scientist and stuck her hand out. "I'm Roxie Michaels. Michaels with an S, and Roxie, never Roxanne. Who in the world are you?"

Mesmer didn't take her hand but smiled all the same. "You can call me Mesmer. That's Mesmer without a Z. If you don't mind, I'm here to chat with Mr. Edison."

Pudge sat. "Whuh?"

"Oh, be quiet," Roxie said, and sat next to Pudge. "Go right ahead," she said to Mesmer.

Mesmer turned to Eddie. "The belt?"

Eddie hesitated and raised his shirt. The belt still hung snug around his waist.

"Excellent. Hand it over."

Even though he had been in possession of the belt for only a matter of hours, Eddie didn't want to give it up. He had felt the same way about the metal nut when Lance and company had tried to take it. Why did these objects have such a hold on him? Because they're part of my birthright, he told himself.

Still, he unbuckled the belt and held it out. Mesmer set about examining every inch. "Yes, mmm, I see..."

Roxie nudged him. "Interesting company you're keeping."

"You don't know the half of it," Eddie said.

Mesmer tossed the belt back to Eddie, an annoyed look on his face. "You didn't fix it?"

"Fix it?"

"Why else would I give it to you?" Mesmer seemed genuinely upset.

"You never told me to fix it," Eddie said.

"I never told you *not* to fix it, did I? How long were your trips? Only two, three minutes?"

"Something like that." Eddie was becoming as annoyed as Mesmer. The man hadn't mentioned anything about repairing the thing, had he? No. He hadn't even given him a clue about what the belt did. But instead of being proud of him, Mesmer seemed disappointed. "I think I did a pretty good job of figuring it out."

Mesmer grabbed his bowling ball from the ball return. "If anything, you've damaged it further. I can't believe you didn't fix it!" He took aim and sent the ball down the alley where it jumped the gutter and took out two pins from the adjoining alley. "I never should have sent out that alert."

Pudge was coming around. "Alert? What alert?"

Mesmer pulled a pen from his shirt pocket. As soon as he did, Eddie could hear that the thing was giving off a *ping-ping-ping*. "This alert. Anything with a mechanical mesh brain within ten miles will hear it."

Horror raised the hairs on Eddie's neck. "You mean... that thing, that monster knows where we are?"

"What monster?" Roxie and Pudge asked in unison.

Mesmer rolled his eyes. "You know the legends about the Jersey Devil? Well, they're all true, but they get one thing wrong. The Jersey Devil wasn't born, it was built. By none other than Vernon Sly to act as his slave and protector."

Eddie was fuming. He raised the belt over his head. “And you’re telling me it wants this?”

Mesmer tilted his head, his face a mix of sympathy and pity. “It would seem so.”

The room was assaulted by the shrill sound of a steam whistle. Eddie froze. The Jersey Devil, the mechanical monstrosity that had come after him back on Echo Island... it was here.

The snack bar exploded in a cloud of candy bars, drywall and wood, and in lurched the metal beast. Its red eyes blazed, its shimmering wings rustled, its clawed hand gripped and opened, gripped and opened. Had the thing been a living creature, it could not be more terrifying than what stood before them.

It scanned the room then locked eyes on the group at lane five. “Oh, no,” Eddie whispered. The thing launched itself toward them, steam streaming from the sides of its metal-toothed mouth.

Eddie turned to Mesmer. “Click us back, click us back!” he screamed. Mesmer just stood there.

“It won’t do any good,” Mesmer said, resigned. “It can obviously shift back and forth as easily as we can.” Was the man actually giving up? Or did he want Eddie to be caught?

Eddie caught Roxie’s eye. “Click. Us. Back!” Roxie caught his meaning and delivered a swift kick to Mesmer’s shin. The man howled in pain. Roxie swiped the clicker out of his hand and tossed it to Eddie.

Eddie pressed the button.

Crack! The crowd of bowlers returned, still eagerly trying for their three strikes in a row. There was no sign of the Jersey Devil...

Zap! The mechanical creature reappeared, still moving at a galloping pace. Kids screamed as the thing clanked forward, knocking them out of the way. Bowling balls went flying as people rushed to get out of its way.

Eddie was transfixed. He didn't even notice Mesmer come up behind him. The man deftly snatched the clicker out of Eddie's hand. "I'd put that belt on if I were you," Mesmer said. And then, with a click, he was gone.

Eddie fumbled to get the belt buckled around his waist, but there wasn't time. The thing was almost on top of him.

Wham! A bowling ball struck the side of the creature's head, knocking it off course. It stumbled past Eddie and toppled over the ball return, metal limbs groaning, whistle shrieking.

What had happened? Eddie turned to find Pudge grabbing for a second bowling ball. "So glad I decided to show up." He hoisted a heavy, multi-colored ball and threw it at the beast. The ball struck the creature in one of its wings, the metal giving off a thunderous, vibrating sound.

"We've got to get out of here," Roxie said pointedly, and she was right. Eddie looked around and saw that almost every kid had made it to the exits. Even the Mustache Mafia was nowhere to be found.

Eddie took advantage of the temporary pause in the action to cinch the belt and buckle it. The lights on the packs were flickering dangerously.

He had to concentrate. If he could slip back just five, no, *ten* minutes ago, he could warn his friends about the Jersey Devil's imminent arrival.

The thing was back on its feet. It turned toward him. Pudge tried cannonballing one more bowling ball its way, but it easily batted it away, sending it hurtling toward Mrs. Branch's office. Eddie thought he heard a muffled cry.

Ten minutes ago, ten minutes. Pudge had just returned with the hotdogs. He *saw* the plate weighted down with the dogs, he *smelled* the onions piled high, he *heard* the crack of bowling balls striking the pins, he *felt* the pinch of his bowling shoes...

Why hadn't he eaten a hotdog?

The Jersey Devil approached. It towered over him. Eddie could hear its inner workings spinning and spitting. Heat came off the thing like a furnace. It opened its massive, mechanical jaws and leaned in as if to swallow him whole.

Imagine the hotdog. Just imagine it! Maybe that'll be good enough!

Eddie threw every bit of concentration into imagining what that hotdog would have tasted like. Its skin, the onions, the mustard-soaked bun. Concentrate. *Concentrate!*

Just as the creature clamped its claws around Eddie's arms, it began to flicker. It was there, it wasn't there, it was there. The beast cocked its head, like Cooper did when puzzled.

He looked over to where Roxie was standing. Or... wasn't standing. She was calling out to him, but he couldn't hear her.

The packs on the belt grew hotter and hotter. He could smell burning metal and plastic, feel the heat start to singe his skin. The whole world began to strobe. But it wasn't the whole world strobing, was it? It was *him*. Whatever mechanism that made the belt work didn't like him trying to fake it out. Eddie was caught in a loop, stuttering back and forth between two different moments in time.

The creature moved closer and then... it moved *through* him. Eddie felt a pressure in his chest as the thing slid through his body, like smoke. For a split second, he could see its insides, see the gears and the pistons and the vacuum tubes that made the infernal thing tick.

And then it was behind him.

The ferocious beast whirled about and tried grabbing at him again. It came up with nothing but air. Eddie grinned, proud of himself, but his smile quickly faded when he saw that the monster had decided to change its tactics.

Moving like lightning, the thing clamped its claw down on Pudge's wrists. With an industrial howl, it spread its metal wings.

"No!" Eddie and Roxie screamed in unison.

The Jersey Devil beat its wings, and a rush of wind hit Eddie in the face as it lifted off the ground, Pudge in tow.

"I didn't really eat a hotdog! Abort! Stop! Stop!" He pounded on the belt. Sparks shot out, shocking his hands. And then, the lights went dark. He had stopped strobing back and forth.

The creature flapped around the bowling alley, its wings catching the ceiling panels, ripping them loose. It ran into hanging lights, pulling them from their moorings. It circled the big room twice and then it soared upward, bashing its way through the roof, taking his screaming friend with it.

Eddie pulled the scalding belt from around his waist and ran to stand underneath the huge hole. The Jersey Devil was already disappearing from view into the late afternoon sky.

Pudge was gone.

CHAPTER ELEVEN

Eddie could hardly breathe. He looked around. He and Roxie were alone in the bowling alley.

"It took him! That thing. Eddie, was that the...? It couldn't have been." Roxie's mind was spinning.

Eddie heard moans coming from Mrs. Branch's office. It seemed she'd survived her run in with the bowling ball. He grabbed the belt and headed over toward the office, a shell-shocked Roxie trailing behind. There lay Mrs. Branch, splayed out in a pile of paperwork. "Can I help you, Mrs. Branch?" he asked.

"If you're leaving, leave the shoes!" she barked.

Eddie and Roxie were only too happy to swap out the painful bowling shoes for their own sneakers, which they had to retrieve from a jumbled pile of smelly shoes. They picked their way through rubble toward the front door but found it blocked by a section of crumbled ceiling. They headed for the side exit instead.

"That was the Jersey Devil, wasn't it, Eddie Edison?" Roxie's astonishment had faded, replaced by the need to understand what just happened.

"Yes, yes," said Eddie. He didn't want to have to explain. He needed to find Mesmer. He needed to figure out what to do next. Still, Roxie pressed him.

"It took him. Pudge is gone. What are you going to do about it?"

Eddie whirled on her. "What am I going to do?" he shouted, all his fear and anger bubbling over. "Well, I don't know! All right? All I know is that this is *my* fault. If I hadn't brought you two into this mess, if I hadn't caught that stupid nut, if I'd never met Mesmer, Pudge would be home right now instead of flying over Lake Mohawk!"

Roxie listened as Eddie continued, his breath coming in short, sharp gasps. "Mesmer!" he spat. "Why did I listen to him, why did I trust him? Because he told me I was special, that's why. That's why!"

Eddie felt dizzy. He ceased his rant and looked at Roxie. She was standing with her head cocked, lip curled. "Who is this guy Mesmer really?" she snarled.

"He's a real jerk!" Eddie said, shoving open the side door and stumbling out into the sunlight. "For all I know, he's the one who took Pudge!" Eddie shouted at the sky. "For all I know *he's* Vernon Sly, that crazy-haired, nutball!"

"I take great offence at that," a voice said above him. "I wouldn't call myself crazy-haired in the least. A bit unkempt, perhaps."

Eddie spun around. There, atop the roof of the bowling alley sat Mesmer. He was kicking his feet back and forth as if he were simply out enjoying the day.

"How's Reggie?" Mesmer asked. "I have missed the little guy."

Eddie was furious. He was about to lay into Mesmer when Roxie stepped in front of him and shouted, "You let that monster take him away! You lured it here and you let it take Pudge!"

"Can't argue with you there," Mesmer said.

Eddie had had enough. He tossed the belt on the ground. "Here, I don't want it. I don't want anything to do with time travel or Mad Scientists or whatever you call my stupid birthright. I just want my friend back!"

"You want him back? Fine. Figure it out. No one's stopping you."

A humorless laugh escaped from Roxie. "I guess you didn't notice the nine-foot tall robot."

"That thing?" Mesmer snorted in reply. "Why didn't Eddie just open up a black hole to suck it in? He's done it before."

"How do you know about that?" Eddie asked, glaring at Mesmer.

"Or why not freeze the fuel that runs through its copper veins? Or disable its visual cortex? You could have, Eddie, you know. If you had stopped and thought about it for a moment."

"Stopped and thought...?" Eddie was through with this guy. "With that metal monster trashing everything around me?"

"The operative word there is metal," Mesmer said, readying to drop down to the ground. "Now, if that had been a real Jersey Devil, you might be out of luck." The man slid off the roof and landed on the ground with a whomp.

"Meaning?" Why didn't Mesmer just come out and say what he meant?

"I stuck years of academic training inside your head. Think about it."

Riddles! Always riddles. "I don't know. I don't know. I don't know!"

"Metal," Roxie said. "Metal means it's manmade."

"Bingo!" crowed Mesmer. "And what one man can *make*, another man can *unmake*."

"But I'm just a kid!" Eddie shouted. "Why didn't *you* unmake that thing when it attacked us, huh? Why didn't you unmake it back on Echo Island?"

Mesmer stepped closer to Eddie. His tone turned serious. "Because I couldn't. Don't ask me to explain. You're just going to have to trust me for now." He looked to Roxie. "Both of you."

Eddie shook his head. "But I don't trust you. Not one bit. Not anymore. Come on, Roxie." He turned and headed for the front of the building to retrieve his bike. "Why did you even look me up in the first place?" he mumbled.

"In part, because I wanted to help you get your father back," said Mesmer.

Eddie stopped in his tracks. "My father? He's alive?"

Eddie looked to Roxie, who looked as shocked as he felt. Mesmer seemed to be weighing very heavily what to say next. "He is. That is, I believe he is. I'm about sixty, sixty-five percent sure."

Roxie raised an eyebrow. "What are you, a weatherman?"

"But you don't know?" Eddie asked.

"No, but what if he is and you do nothing," said Mesmer. "Could you live with yourself knowing there was a chance and you just walked away?"

"It's Sly, isn't it?" Eddie shuddered. "He found some way to survive the flood and travel to the present. And you think that if my dad's alive, Sly's got him. Right?"

"I do. So, what do you say? Are you up to it?"

Eddie considered this but didn't answer. He looked past Roxie at the crowd of kids milling about in the parking lot in front of the bowling alley. Some were crying into phones asking for rides home, others were recounting the attack with wild gestures.

Mesmer stepped up behind him. "When I talk about your birthright, I'm not trying to convince you that you're any better than anyone else. No, you're neither better nor worse. But you see those kids over there? Not one of them can do what you can, and that includes getting your father back. I think it's everyone's duty to become the person they were meant to be. Am I wrong?"

Eddie looked at Mesmer, then to Roxie. "Do you trust him?"

"Not a bit," Roxie said, "but a sixty percent chance is nothing to sneeze at."

"Maybe sixty-five," Mesmer said hopefully.

Eddie caved. "You didn't happen to have a plan to get my dad back, did you?"

Mesmer smiled. "Let's say someone at your school has something you want. A new backpack or an oscillating detonator."

Roxie shook her head. "I'm pretty sure they wouldn't let anyone into our school with an oscillating detonator..."

"Don't interrupt. How would you go about getting it from them?"

Eddie thought for a moment. "I'd have to give them something they'd want more."

Mesmer clapped his hands together. "Double Bingo!"

Eddie looked down. He was still holding the belt. "This. If I can fix this, I can trade this for Dad."

"Maybe," said Mesmer. "It's a long shot, but I think it's... well, I know it's the only one we've got."

The belt was toast. The leather was scorched, the packs were cracked, loose parts tinkled inside when he so much as moved it. Only one of the packs showed any signs of life – a dim glimmer of energy peeked out like a flashlight on its last legs. "You think I can fix it?"

Mesmer grinned. "I think if anyone can, you can."

Roxie stamped her foot impatiently. "Great. You're all on the same team. Fantastic. Has everyone forgotten about Pudge? He's probably halfway to Pennsylvania by now."

"Let's go back to my house. I just hope I can find the right parts in Dad's workshop."

"Oh," said Mesmer, shaking his head. "You won't find what you need there. This belt depends on old technology, old parts. You can't just put it back together with a transistor radio and a spool of wire."

Eddie was stumped. Where did the man expect him to find the parts he needed? He didn't have to ask. "You'll need to get into the old lab."

"And just where is the old lab?" Eddie asked.

"Where else?" Mesmer chortled. "At the bottom of the lake!"

Eddie's hope evaporated. "You've got to be kidding me."

"Nope," said Mesmer. "Remember my presentation about the flooding of Voltaic Valley, how Sly wiped out the town leaving it and its people deep at the bottom of a newly formed lake? That town is still down there. And the only building fitted with pressurized windows and doors?"

"The old lab?"

"Precisely!" said Mesmer. "Big, hulking place with smokestacks on either end. You can't miss it."

The wild-haired man turned as if to leave. "Wait! How do I get down there? Mesmer, wait!"

The man stopped. "All right, I'll give you a jumpstart." He rummaged around in his pockets, pulled out two objects and handed them to Eddie.

"What's that?" Roxie asked.

"A transistor radio and a spool of wire. Good luck! If you need any help, I'll be there in a shot. I promise." And with that, Mesmer pulled his keychain from his pocket, clicked it and disappeared.

"He did say at the bottom of the lake, didn't he?" said Roxie. "The *bottom*? How on earth does he expect us to..."

Eddie held up a finger to cut her off. This was no time for doubt. Either he moved forward or fear, worry, all those nasty emotions that gummed up the works would... well, gum up the works. He pocketed the radio and wire, threw the belt over his shoulder.

"Come on," Eddie said. "Let's go get Pudge."

He headed for the parking lot. "Eddie? Eddie! Hey! Slow down!" Roxie said as she sprinted to catch up.

The crowd had thinned some, but not much. Kids were taking selfies of themselves in front of the bowling alley, making sure they could prove to their friends that they were there when the Jersey Devil had struck.

Lance was standing next to his car, trying to convince his mustached buddies to stick around. Hedges looked like he was eager to get home, and Babcock looked like he was about to throw up. Yup, worrying didn't look good on anyone.

Eddie and Roxie approached the bike rack. Eddie was glad to see his bike was still there.

"Did you guys see it?" a trembling voice said, and Eddie turned to see Jimmy Ticks sitting astride his own bike. The mustard smear had stained his shirt. "The monster? Did you see it?"

"I did," said Eddie.

"I'm never going bowling again," Jimmy whimpered.

"I'm with you there, kid," Roxie said.

Something about Jimmy's bike caught Eddie's eye. It was festooned with reflectors and bike lamps – apparently either Jimmy or Jimmy's mom *really* wanted him to stand out in traffic. What was it about those lights?

A deflated mylar birthday balloon rustled by, and Eddie caught it with his foot. The bike lamps, the balloon, the radio, the wire... Eddie's mind lit up with the possibilities. He looked quickly around. He only needed one more thing, just one more thing.

His eyes lighted on Lance's car. A bell went off in his head. With its convertible top and streamlined shape, it was perfect.

Jimmy started to pedal off. "Jimmy!" Eddie cried. "Come back here!"

Jimmy, like most kids who were used to enduring a daily barrage of spitballs and insults, flinched at the sound of Eddie's voice. He almost fell off his bike. "Why?"

"Oh, come on," Roxie moaned. "We just got rid of him."

"Just come here," Eddie continued, recognizing Jimmy's reticence and shifting to a calmer, friendlier voice.

The nervous boy walked his bike back over to the bike rack. "What do you want?"

"I need you to do us a favor."

"What kind of favor?"

Eddie paused. How would the kid react? "We need you to go over to Lance and his friends and lure them away from his car."

At first, Jimmy just laughed, but when he saw that Eddie was serious, he turned pale. "No way!"

"Please, Jimmy!" Eddie searched his pockets. "I'll give you a dollar."

"I wouldn't even look their way for a dollar!"

Eddie reached deeper and came up with a ten. "How about ten, no, eleven dollars?"

"Keep your money."

"Come on, Eddie," Roxie said, trying to pulling him away. "Tick tock, tick tock."

Eddie shrugged her off and glanced over at Lance, who was getting his car keys out. Soon, it would be too late.

"I'll do it if you'll be my friends," Jimmy said.

"Huh?" Eddie said.

"Say what?" asked Roxie.

"I don't have any. Friends, I mean. If you guys *promise* you'll be my friends, I'll distract them."

Eddie didn't quite know what to say. "Sure," he blurted out. "Sounds good."

Roxie threw Eddie an incredulous look but kept her mouth shut.

With resolve, Jimmy Ticks set his bike back in the rack, turned toward the Mustache Mafia and marched forward as if he was going to his doom.

"What's the plan, genius?" Roxie asked.

"If we want to get Pudge, we'll need some wheels."

Roxie followed Eddie's gaze to Lance's car. "We're dead," she said.

Quickly, Eddie reached down and snagged the mylar balloon. Then, he grabbed ahold of the largest of Jimmy's bike lamps. "Sorry, Jimmy," he said under his breath as he wrenched the lamp free.

Laughter rose in the distance.

"At least we'll have company," Roxie said. "Those guys are going to massacre him."

Eddie looked. A group of kids had surrounded Jimmy who was stumbling about. Babcock had stopped looking so sick and motioned to Lance and Hedges, alerting them of the entertainment.

He looked closer. What in the world? The kid had tied his own shoes together and was tripping himself up like he was half asleep.

Eddie's heart sank. Was that the only way the poor kid could cause a distraction? He felt for Jimmy, really he did, but he had a job to do. Now, if Lance would just take the bait.

"I know babies who can walk better than you!" Lance shouted, and a whole new wave of laughter swept through the crowd.

"Yeah! You're a baby!" Hedges added. Babcock socked him in the arm.

Eddie was coiled like a spring, ready to make a dash for the car. "As soon it's clear, follow me," he said. "We'll have to be fast."

"I don't do fast, remember," Roxie said, grinding her mismatched sneakers into the gravel.

Jimmy tripped and went down on his knees. Lance just couldn't resist. "Here, lemme help the baby up!" He walked over to Jimmy, who now looked to be in *way* over his head, the rest of the Mustache Mafia right behind.

"Now!" Eddie said and bolted. He caught Roxie off guard, and with her first steps she did a pretty good imitation of Jimmy Ticks, stumbling over her own feet. Eddie raced ahead to Lance's car, tossed the belt into the backseat, leapt over the door and hunkered down behind the wheel.

A few seconds later, Roxie toppled into the car with him, all gangly arms and legs. "Sorry!" she said.

It took a moment for Eddie to extract himself from her flailing limbs, but when he did, he reached down and yanked the car radio from the dashboard, ripping out its guts.

"That clinches it," Roxie said. "Pudge officially has a better chance of seeing tomorrow than we do."

Eddie tore the balloon in half and quickly wrapped it tightly with wire. He reached under the dashboard and pulled an important looking wire free. His hands flew, twisting wires, attaching transistors, creating what he was seeing in his mind.

"Hey, Lance!" a thick voice shouted. "Someone's in your car!" It was Hedges.

Roxie poked her head up. Lance, who had been trotting Jimmy Ticks around like he was some sort of puppet, dropped the kid and went on high alert. "Who is that?" he bellowed.

Eddie's hands worked faster and faster. Almost there...

The Mustache Mafia headed toward the car. "Now would definitely be a time to motor, Eddie," screeched Roxie.

Eddie reached for the ignition. No key.

A strong hand reached out and grabbed Eddie around the collar. "What do you think you're doing, munch?" Lance growled.

"I was... I... I..." No words. Eddie had no words.

Just then, someone landed in Roxie's lap. She let out a cry as she realized it was Jimmy. "What are you doing, Ticks? Get off of me!"

Jimmy smiled at Eddie, and it was strange, that smile. There was pure joy in it. The kid was about to be pummeled by the Mustache Mafia, and he was loving every minute of it.

His next action explained everything. Jimmy reached over, slid a key into the ignition and turned it. "Drive!"

Eddie didn't stop to think. He threw the car into reverse the way he'd seen his father do a hundred times, and the car lurched backward. His shirt tore, a swatch of it coming loose in Lance's grip.

"Get 'em!" Lance screamed. He and his buddies rushed the car.

Eddie shifted into drive. The car protested his abrupt flooring of the gas pedal, but it moved forward.

"Faster!" Roxie shouted, struggling to shift Jimmy off of her.

"Whoo!" Jimmy hooted as he tumbled into the backseat.

Eddie eased off the gas a touch, and the car responded by giving him the speed he wanted. He sped out of the parking lot, away from the bowling alley, leaving Lance roaring behind him. The car leapt over a lane divider, and soon, Eddie and company were barreling down the road to the lake.

"How'd you get the keys?" Eddie asked, dodging traffic.

"It was easy. I just snuck them out of his pocket when he lifted me upside-down," Jimmy said, proudly.

Eddie swerved, barely missing the Lake Mohawk sign at the top of the hill leading down to the water. Men busy painting new lines on the road scattered as Eddie sped toward the boardwalk.

"Aren't you going to slow down?" Jimmy's temporary bravery was evaporating.

The car vaulted onto the boardwalk, taking out a mailbox. Startled tourists leapt aside.

"Eddie," Roxie warned.

"Eddie?" Jimmy shrieked.

Eddie knew he had to time this just right. He turned to Roxie. "Hold the wheel!"

Roxie grabbed the wheel, jerking the car toward traffic. "Hold it steady!" Eddie said as he bent down and twisted two final wires together. He felt a short shock and every bit of metal in the car began to hum.

He sat back up and took the wheel. "Jimmy! When I say three, I want you to jump. Can you do that, Jimmy?"

"Wha...?" Jimmy went white.

Eddie had no time to wait – he floored it. "One..." The car zoomed straight for the wooden railing. "Two..." The car struck the railing, shattering it and flew out over the water. "Three!"

Jimmy jumped, his momentum sending him skipping across the water like a stone. Eddie and Roxie braced for impact as the car plunged into Lake Mohawk.

CHAPTER TWELVE

The car groaned as it hit the water, threatening to break apart. The black depths swallowed the vehicle as it plummeted downward. The sunlight grew dimmer and dimmer as Eddie and Roxie sank. The air bubble that had enveloped the sports car held, though Eddie feared that it would burst at any second.

"Remarkable," Roxie whispered as they sank. "Just remarkable."

When the wheels hit the rocky lakebed, Eddie realized that he had been holding his breath. He let it out with a whoosh so powerful that it set the air bubble wobbling all around them.

"Easy, Breathy McBreatherson," Roxie scolded.

"Sorry."

The makeshift device Eddie had fashioned to create the bubble was crudely cobbled together. No telling how long it would keep the water at bay. He would have to move fast. He fumbled around for the headlights and switched them on just in time to catch a startled turtle swimming past. It ducked its head and veered off into the shadows.

"Which way?" Roxie asked.

"We went into the water heading south," said Eddie, "and the car didn't turn while we sank. I think if we go straight, we'll be driving toward the deepest part of the lake. If there really *is* an old town down here, that's where it would be."

"And if it's *not* down here?" Roxie clicked her fingernails together nervously.

Eddie couldn't even consider that. "It's got to be." He pressed down on the gas, and the car lurched forward. The way was rocky. The car bumped and jolted as it drove on.

"What do you get when you cross a frog and a bunny?" Roxie asked.

"What?"

"I said, what do you get..."

Eddie shook his head. "Are you seriously telling jokes right now?"

Roxie shrugged. "I thought it might calm you down."

"I'm calm!" Eddie said as the car hit a particularly large rock. The force of it lifted the car's left side up off its wheels, and the two of them braced for disaster. After teetering for what seemed like forever, the car slowly sank back onto all four tires and continued forward.

"No more jokes," Eddie ordered.

Roxie held her tongue for as long she could. "A ribbit. You get a ribbit."

The view ahead was murky. Eddie couldn't see more than twenty feet ahead of him. They passed a sunken canoe, a rusted outboard motor, an artificial Christmas tree that the wind must have stolen from someone's dock.

Eddie was beginning to despair of finding anything but junk at the bottom of the lake when they came upon a lamppost. It jutted up out of the muck – an old, gas-powered light, ornate in design.

As they drove on, they passed another. And another. Then, the remains of some sort of shop appeared on their left. No, not big enough for a shop. It was a small seller's stand, a place where he could imagine someone peddling newspapers, fruit or the like. A weathered sign swung back and forth with the current.

"Dr. Lipsing's Lamps and Levers," Roxie read aloud. "There's Carter's Chemicals. And Prof. Parnell's Pistons and Pumps."

"I guess in a town filled with Mad Scientists, spare parts would be pretty popular," Eddie said.

"Yeah, that and alliteration."

"Huh?"

"Nothing," Roxie sighed.

The car gave one final thump and leveled off. "I think we're on a street," said Eddie. "An actual street."

Houses peered at them from the shadows. Big structures that bent this way and that, twisted under the deep water currents of the lake.

Eddie could imagine what this place must have looked like back before Sly had flooded the valley, wiping the Mad Scientists from memory. He saw men in top hats sporting canes, women in fancy dresses, like in those old movies his mother liked to watch after a long day recording diet pill commercials. All of them smiling, discussing their latest inventions, debating scientific theories.

All gone. Nothing but their dilapidated homes to show they were ever here.

The car coughed.

"What are you doing?" Roxie asked. "Don't slow down."

"I'm not doing anything," Eddie snapped, but he quickly realized that he had been pressing down on the accelerator too hard – a nervous reaction to the thought of all those long-dead ancestors. He eased off, but just a bit. The effort it took the car to slog through the water must be taxing its engine.

"Don't worry," he said. "As long as we don't run out of gas, we're fine."

Roxie leaned in front of him, blocking his view as she checked the gas gauge. His face was instantly buried in her tangle of red hair.

"Roxie!"

She shifted back to her seat, her face pale. Eddie looked at the dashboard, eyes searching for the gas gauge. Speedometer, temperature gauge, turn signals... ah! There it was.

Eddie's heart skipped a beat. The arrow was quivering just above *E*. That cough had been a warning – the gas tank was almost empty.

"Lance, you cheap...!" Eddie sputtered, but he had to quickly turn the wheel to avoid the remains of a statue that loomed up in their path, sprawled in the middle of the street.

Eddie couldn't see the thing very clearly as they swerved past, but he saw enough. It was a statue of a man wearing a coat and vest, his arm upraised, a light bulb in his hand.

"That's..." Roxie whispered.

"Thomas Edison."

The engine coughed again, and sparks lit up the dashboard. The scent of burning metal filled the car's interior. The car shuddered and came to stop, the engine gasping for fuel while Thomas Edison's sculpted face peered in at Eddie through his window.

The air bubble retracted a good three inches all around them. Eddie froze. "No sudden movements," he warned.

"No problem," Roxie said.

Curious fish, no doubt attracted by the jerky movements of the soon-to-be-dead sports car, clustered around the flickering headlights.

Eddie started to panic. If the engine died, his device would fail. If the device failed, the bubble would burst. If the bubble burst...

There was no getting around it. This was the end of the road. The end of everything – school, friends, the hope of ever seeing his mother again, the hope of ever finding his father. *Cooper.* What was that lunk of a dog going to do without him? For some reason it was the thought of Cooper waiting patiently at the door for him that brought tears to his eyes.

"No, no, no," Roxie said, shaking him. "Don't you clock out. Fix it. Do that thing you do and fix it!"

Eddie didn't respond. He leaned forward and looked up through the windshield at the surface of the lake high above. How far away was it? Forty, fifty feet? When the water came rushing into the car, would they be able to withstand its onslaught, open a window, wriggle free and make it to the surface before their lungs ran out of air?

"Fix it!" Roxie pleaded.

Outside the bubble, the fish continued to stare into the headlights, like gawkers at the scene of an accident.

"Go on. Git! Git!" he shouted. The fish remained.

In the midst of his fear and terror of being swallowed up by Lake Mohawk, his annoyance at the fish welled up inside him. It was one thing to fail, but to fail with an audience?

Eddie reached for the light switch and toggled it, flashing the car's brights into the fish's eyes. It worked. The fish scattered, no doubt in search of dimmer surroundings.

"Wait! What was that?" Roxie asked.

Eddie squinted. He flicked the brights on again and there it was, barely visible in the distance. A towering brick smokestack. Eddie's mind raced. What exactly was it that Mesmer had told him?

"Big, hulking place with smokestacks on either end. You can't miss it."

"The old lab!" Eddie shouted. "We found it! And it can't be more than thirty yards ahead."

The car hiccupped. More sparks spat from beneath the dash landing on Eddie's shoes. The air bubble buckled on Roxie's side, water trickling down the window.

"I know this is a terrible time to say this," Roxie blurted out, "but I failed every single swim class I ever took."

Eddie caught his reflection in the rearview mirror and saw the fear in his eyes. "Come on!" he barked at himself. "Think, Eddie. Think! THINK!"

Crack! Suddenly, it felt like a miniature bolt of lightning struck the center of his brain, splitting it in half. The shock was unlike anything Eddie had ever experienced. The electrical jolt he'd gotten from the metal nut was a playful tap compared with the wallop his mind received in that instant.

"Look!" cried Roxie.

Outside the car, the light bulb in the statue's hand began to glow. Dim at first but getting brighter and brighter, until it promised to illuminate the entire lake.

A question leapt into Eddie's mind. Not in a voice he could hear or in words he could see but simply a calmly formed thought. "Where are you?"

"Where am I?" Eddie shook his head. "I'm at the bottom of the lake, where do you think I am?"

"What'd you say?" asked Roxie.

Just as dispassionately, a second question popped into his head. "Where *specifically* are you?"

Who or what was asking these questions? The sound of glass cracking as the passenger side window pressed inward convinced him he had no choice but to answer.

"I'm sitting behind the wheel of a convertible trapped in an artificially created air bubble stalled on a street at the bottom of Lake Mohawk about thirty yards from the old lab."

"Tell me something I don't know!" Roxie shouted.

Eddie waited. As the seconds ticked by with no response, no further questions, he began to panic. The trickle of water had grown into a torrent. Soon the water would rise up into the makeshift wiring of the device and the bubble would pop...

The light bulb in the statue's hand pulsed. "How will you get from where you are to where you want to be without drowning?"

Eddie was dumbfounded. "If I knew that, what would I need all these questions for?"

And then... just as soon as he had asked the question, he knew the answer. The answer trotted into his head like a friendly dog.

Pressure!

His mind leapt back to a Christmas morning when he was much, much younger. Cooper, only a puppy then, was sniffing around in the pile of presents under the tree, a bright red bow around his neck. Eddie's father, a towering figure to one so young, leaned down and handed him a gift.

"Open it up, Sport," he said.

Eddie's tiny hands ripped at the wrapping paper and pulled out an object made of wood.

The memory began to fade, and Eddie concentrated. *Concentrate.* The thing in his hands sharpened, took form. He could see it now. It was a...

Pop gun. A wooden pop gun. He saw himself draw the handle back from the shaft and press back down. *Pop!* The cap at the end went flying.

The light bulb in the statue's hand dimmed and went dark, and Eddie jolted back to the present.

"That's it!"

"What's it?" Roxie howled. She had crawled up onto her seat to avoid the rising water, her hair pressing dangerously against the surface of the bubble.

"There's tons of water pressure pushing down on this air bubble," Eddie said. "If I can redirect that pressure in one direction, lining it up *behind* us, it could shoot this car forward. Maybe even enough to reach the old lab."

"How in the world would you do that... Ah!" A minnow leapt from the water below and landed in her hair. "Fish!"

Ignoring Roxie's flailing efforts to extract the little fish, Eddie scrunched down to examine the makeshift device he had fashioned below the dash. It was lighting up like a sparkler, but if he reversed the black and red wires, threw the car into neutral before grounding the electrical net with the car's key...

"I'm only going to have one shot at this," he thought. He reached back, grabbed the belt and buckled it about his waist. If this was going to work, he'd better be ready.

Launching into action, he let his fingers obey his brain, twisting, reconfiguring. He shifted the car into neutral. Immediately, the air bubble collapsed. The water had the car in its grip.

But not *all* of the car. One paltry air pocket remained wrapped around both Eddie and Roxie. They were inside a bubble inside the car.

Roxie was trying to say something, but every time she opened her mouth, the inner surface of the bubble threatened to burst. She opted for silence.

Eddie was making his last adjustments when an odd sound from the rear of the car caught his attention and he whirled around. The rear edge of the bubble was, well, bubbling. Like when you blow air into a soda. A flurry of froth fizzed, ready to...

Boom! An explosion of bubbles propelled the car forward. Instantly, it began to veer off course. Eddie had to grip the wheel tight to get the thing back on track. He zeroed in on the smokestack and held on for all he was worth.

The initial thrust sent the car hurtling toward the old lab, and Eddie was happy for that. What *didn't* make him so happy was when the car began to slowly crawl to a stop.

They were five feet from the old lab when the bubble burst. Five feet away when the weight of Lake Mohawk settled down onto the car. Like the rest of the debris scattered across the lakebed, it was never to see the light of day again.

Luckily for Eddie, he was two steps ahead of the game. In the moments before the water rushed in, he yanked his device from under the dashboard and, with a speed that surprised even him, wired it to the last remaining energized pack on the belt. Suddenly, he was safe and sound inside his own mini-bubble.

He reached for Roxie's arm, but all his hand found was her hair. The bubble retracted around him, leaving just his arm outside its protective shell. His arm... and Roxie.

For a second, their eyes locked. Eddie watched helplessly as Roxie thrashed about, her expression wild with fear as she struggled to hold her breath. In moments, she lost the fight, and the last of her air escaped, rising up to the surface. Abandoning her.

No! I killed her!

When the water had swallowed the car, it also swallowed its battery. The headlights blinked out. The only light Eddie had to navigate by was the dim glow from the belt. Nevertheless, he stepped forward, hauling his friend's limp body along with him.

Holding tight to Roxie's hair kept Eddie from floating upward but also made moving forward a battle. His heart was pounding in his ears by the time he reached the outer brick wall of the lab. He looked up. Towering over him stood the smokestack silhouetted against the surface above. He'd made it.

Now what? A door. There *had* to be a door somewhere. He sidestepped, careful not to run his feet into any stray rocks, and accidentally knocked Roxie's head against a sunken log. He knew that, should he trip and go tumbling, the improvised contraption keeping the bubble about him would likely fail, releasing his precious air.

He thrust his free arm out of the bubble as well and ran his hand along the brick, his fingers searching out any sign of an entrance. Finally, his hand lit upon a metal slab set into the masonry. He judged its width and was quite certain he had found the door he was looking for.

His suspicions were confirmed, but where one would normally find a doorknob, there was nothing.

"It must only open from the inside!" Eddie despaired. How long had Roxie gone without air? *Too long.*

He pounded his fist against the door again and again, more out of frustration than any hope that his actions would accomplish anything.

To his surprise and delight, the door began to move. It pivoted in the middle, and as it did so, a wall of water slammed him forward. Eddie rushed forward in a swirl of water, tumbling and turning, his protective air bubble scattered, Roxie's limp body pulled from his grip.

In a flash, it was over. The door thudded closed. The water that had carried them into the place was quickly draining away into the grated floor beneath him. Eddie was weak, slopping wet and had no clue as to how he ever hoped to get back up to the surface in one piece.

Eddie looked down at Roxie. Her skin was blue.

"Roxie!" he shouted. Then, as he'd learned in summer camp (or was it something Mesmer had stuck in his head?), he cleared Roxie's airway, pinched her nose, tilted her head back and *breathed* into her mouth.

After five enormous lungsful of air, Eddie was starting to fear the worst when a gurgling spurt of air and water burst from her mouth along with a very surprised minnow. The little fish hit the floor, flipped about and disappeared down the grate.

"You're alive!" Eddie cheered.

Roxie sat up, her jaw askew, her hair a wet mess about her face. She gingerly felt the spot on the top of her head where Eddie had gripped her hair during the trek underwater. "I think I might be permanently bald on top."

"Well," Eddie said half laughing, half crying. "If anyone can pull that look off, it's you."

Eddie helped her to her feet. Once they were up, they turned to look at the room around them.

Room? No. It was as big as a warehouse or an airplane hangar. Eddie had once been to New York's Grand Central Station and there was something about this place that reminded him of that Manhattan landmark. A fraction of the size, of course, but still.

Ceilings reached up high above with metal girders zigzagging back and forth. Enormous windows that looked out at nothing but the depths of Lake Mohawk. A smooth marble floor and mural-covered walls that seemed to glow. As a matter of fact, they *were* glowing. That accounted for the light that filled the place without a single light bulb to be seen.

Around the periphery of the room sat large metal worktables piled high with equipment. The individual stations reminded Eddie of Mesmer's workspace, although these were as tidy as Mesmer's was chaotic.

The old lab. This must be where they made all of their amazing discoveries, those Mad Scientists. Where scientific mysteries were solved, and wild notions were brought to life.

"I hope they left us a few spare parts," Eddie said, dispelling the sense of awe that had settled over him. "Lemme get this belt fixed, and we'll get out of here."

"What parts are you looking for, exactly?" Roxie asked as they headed further into the room. "Or is this one of your I'll-know-it-when-I-see-it sort of deals?"

"One of those," Eddie said. He spied a particularly cluttered table and made a beeline for it. It was covered with boxes of glass cylinders, spools of wire, piles of disassembled, dust-covered machines. Roxie helped him clear a space to work, and Eddie removed the belt and set it on the table.

The belt had truly been through the wringer, all water-soaked and burnt-out. Was this really what he hoped to trade Sly for his father?

"Stop thinking so much and get to work," Roxie said. He caught her looking at him and could swear she'd just read his mind.

"That guy Sly will probably laugh in my face once he sees this."

"No, he won't," Roxie assured him. "Because you're going fix it and set everything right."

"Yes, I do believe he will," echoed a voice from the far side of the room.

Eddie turned, trying to locate the voice's source. A man stepped into the light. Aside from the cane he sported, there was no denying who the man was.

"Dad?" Eddie gasped.

Chapter Thirteen

It was all Eddie could do to keep from racing across the room. Instead he pressed his back against the workbench and stared at the man before him.

"Is it really you?" he asked.

His father chuckled. "I could ask you the same thing, son."

That laugh! How Eddie had missed it. He threw aside the belt and his caution and rushed into his father's arms.

"Careful," his father said. "Squeeze me any harder and you're likely to break me in two."

Eddie looked up at him. He was haggard, his chin rough with whiskers, but it was him. It was his father.

Eddie turned back to Roxie. He was grinning like a fool. "This is Roxie. Roxie, this is my dad."

Roxie stepped forward to shake Eddie's father's hand, but her sleeves had stretched so much that she was only able to offer him a handful of wet sweater.

Bill Edison regarded his son. "I'm sure you have a lot of questions."

Eddie sure did. "Where have you been? How did you get here?" The words tumbled out of him. "Why do you have a cane? How did you hurt your leg? Where's Sly? What's going on?"

His father shook his head. "Don't I get a hello first?" Eddie squeezed him again.

"Sit," Bill Edison said to his son, motioning to an old wooden chair next to the workbench. "Let me enlighten you." Eddie did as he was told. Nervous, excited and happy all at once, he clasped his hands in front of him to keep them from fidgeting.

Roxie stood apart, feeling somewhat awkward, as if embarrassed by the waves of emotion passing back and forth between father and son. She moved closer to the workbench and poked through a box of springs and gears.

Eddie's father waved his arm at the large room. "You asked where I've been. Well, you're looking at it. Ever since the night I was taken, I've been here in this desolate place. How did I get here? I was dragged here by that maniac's mechanical henchman. The devil, he calls it. The Jersey Devil. Make no mistake about it – the only devil around here is Sly himself."

"How can that be, Dad? Mesmer told me the story about the flood. How can he be here? Now?"

"That is a question I have no answer to, I'm afraid. Suffice it to say that he *is* here," said his father.

"Where?" Eddie glanced around nervously.

"Out hunting down that friend of yours. That Mesmer fellow. He talks about him endlessly. I think it irks him that he can't figure out who the man is."

"To tell you the truth, neither can I," said Eddie.

His father winced at that. "Sly hates having any blind spots. And when he gets frustrated he takes it out on me. A day without food, perhaps, or another in the dark. Petty punishments from a petty man."

"But why did he take you in the first place? And why has he kept you for so long?" Eddie felt close to tears.

Eddie's father nodded toward the belt on the table. "It seems to have something to do with that. I take it you know what it is?"

"It's a time travel belt," Roxie interjected. She realized she should have let Eddie answer, but staying silent just wasn't in her nature.

"Clever friends you keep, son. But do either of you know where it came from?" His father waited for an answer.

Eddie hadn't thought about that. He had been too concerned about getting down here, getting it fixed to ponder the belt's origin. "I suppose it came from down here in the old lab."

His father nodded. "True. But whose brainchild is it? Who conjured it up from their imagination, designed it and fashioned it into the device you now possess?"

Eddie hazarded a guess. "Sly?"

His father's eye twitched violently. What had the man done to his father to make him react so at the mere mention of his name?

"No. That honor falls to none other than Mr. Thomas Edison himself."

"I don't understand," said Eddie. "If he invented time travel way back in the olden days, why don't we know about it? Like the light bulb or his other inventions?"

His father walked over to the table and placed his hand on the belt. "It was the one invention the Mad Scientists deemed too dangerous to allow to exist. Edison was always fixated on the *how* of his inventions and never the *why*. In most cases it didn't matter to the rest of them, but this time they all vowed to destroy it so that it would never fall into the hands of those who might use it... unwisely."

"Like Sly?" Roxie asked.

Eddie's father turned to her and smiled. "Yes. Like Sly." As he took a step toward Eddie, he stumbled and had to catch himself with his cane.

"What happened to your leg?" Eddie asked, concerned.

"Broken," said his father, "by that metal beast when he snatched me away. I had to set the bone myself, splint it myself. Oh, it's healed up, but it's never going to be the same. Nor will I."

The mournful look on his father's face made Eddie wish he knew what to say. Instead of saying a word, Eddie grabbed the belt and held it out. "Let's just smash this thing, and go home. Okay, Dad? Please?"

Bill Edison looked down at the belt and slowly pushed it back toward Eddie. "No, son."

"Why not?"

"If we destroy it, Sly will fix it. If we hide the pieces, he'll find them. And once he has a working belt in his possession, there's no telling what he'll do with it. No. I say we fix it up and use it *ourselves*."

"Use it how?" Eddie asked.

A wry smile spread across his father's face. "Imagine if we were to travel back to the moment Sly snatched me away. Only this time, we were ready for him. We'd stop his scheme before it even had a chance to commence!"

Eddie smiled back. "Do you really think we can do it?"

"With two Edisons on the job? Absolutely."

Eddie welcomed the chance to work beside his father in silence. He felt like every word out of his mouth was a question when really all he wanted to say was how much he had missed him and how incredible it felt to see him once again.

The two busied themselves taking the belt apart, laying out each component in a line so that putting it back together would be less of a chore. Seeing how Roxie squirmed, watching over their shoulders, Eddie gave her the task of making sure each part was tallied and accounted for. Relieved to have a job, she grabbed a notepad and pencil and got to work.

When the belt lay in pieces, deconstructed before them, Eddie's father took it in, a puzzled expression on his face. "I can't make heads or tails of it," he said, the hint of frustration underneath.

To Eddie, the whole of it *instantly* made sense. It was like being on chapter two of a book and suddenly knowing how the whole thing would end.

He also noticed something odd. Although both he and his father were working on the belt together, he got the distinct impression that *he* was taking the lead, *he* was guiding his father through the repair rather than the other way around.

"Hand me that coil," he'd say, and his father would obey. "Toss me those conductors," he'd say, and his father would oblige. He had never felt so sure of himself before. His hands moved like lightning. He improvised and adapted as he reworked the inner configuration of the time travel belt.

Roxie struggled to keep track of the traffic patterns of the pieces. She'd warn Eddie when he ignored a bit of wire or substituted a tube from the belt with one from the pile on the table. Still, Eddie plowed ahead, tweaking the design, making alterations, fixing flaws.

He didn't know how much time had passed since they'd started repairing the belt, but now Eddie noticed that the light outside the large windows had disappeared.

He held up the belt. "Almost done. Just a few more adjustments and it will be good as new. Better maybe."

His father cocked his head. "Better? How better?" It was odd. Something in his father's voice caught him off guard.

Roxie held up a handful of parts. "What about these?" She seemed a bit upset, as if her job of keeping track of the order of things had just been proven to be unnecessary busy work.

"Don't worry about it," Eddie reassured them. "Let's just say I added a few upgrades."

His father put his hand on his shoulder. "That's wonderful. We'll show that Sly who's the boss, eh, son?" Eddie felt himself shy away from his father's touch. But why?

"Hey, Dad?" Eddie wasn't sure what he was going to ask.

"Yes?"

"When I was out there underwater, trying to find my way in here, I came across a statue toppled over in the street."

His father looked perplexed. "And?"

"I'm pretty certain it was a statue of Thomas Edison. And he had a light bulb clasped in his hand."

Eddie's father's eye twitched. "Is there a point to this story, son?"

Eddie looked to Roxie. She was regarding him curiously, head cocked, brow furrowed. If he could just get her alone for a minute, he could ask if she too had felt the mood in the room shift.

"We were stuck out there," said Eddie. "I mean, *really* stuck. I thought we'd never find our way in here. Then, something remarkable happened. The light bulb it, well, it lit up and *boom*! My brain was flooded with questions. Questions that helped me find a way out of that mess."

His father turned away. "The bulb is a brainstormer, one of Edison's little devices. A gift to this community. He set it atop his own statue so that others might benefit from its use. Or so the story goes."

"So, it asks you questions," Roxie said, "to help you solve your problem?"

"It does." Bill Edison stepped closer to Eddie. "And do *you* have a problem in need of solving, son?

"Yes, I do." Eddie tried to swallow, but his mouth had gone dry. "I'm wondering why you've been calling me son when you used to always call me Sport."

His father's eyes narrowed. "What would you imagine the brainstormer would say?"

"I think it would ask, 'What does your gut tell you?'" asked Eddie.

"Your reply?" His father gripped his cane tightly.

Eddie didn't want to answer, but it was too late to hide his suspicions. "That you *aren't* my father."

The man before him raised his cane high over his head and brought it down onto the floor with an electric *crack*. An earsplitting whistle filled the air in response, and in that horrible instant, Eddie knew he was right.

A blinding flash of light lit up the room followed by a gust of wind that swirled about, knocking over chairs, scattering pieces of equipment. A distortion grew in the center of the room, a bending of space that looked like rippling water. Eddie watched open-mouthed as something stepped *through* the ripples, appearing out of thin air.

"Pudge!" Roxie cried.

Pudge gripped his head as if the trip back from the time between seconds had shaken his marbles. Standing behind him, holding him tight was Sly's lumbering, metal beast. *The Jersey Devil.*

"Good to see you again, my mechanical friend!" the man chortled. He walked over to where the monstrosity held Eddie's friend captive. "It would seem Mr. Edison has riddled us out."

Pudge stepped forward, but the metal beast hauled him back. "Eddie! He's not your father! He's...!"

"I know," said Eddie. "He's Vernon Sly." He stared at the copy of his father. "Aren't you?"

"Guilty," said Sly. "Of that and a good many other things."

"Why do you look like my father?"

Sly laughed. "There's a tale in that!"

Pudge pulled free of the Jersey Devil's grip, his shirt ripping. "Don't listen to him, Eddie! Run! I can handle this joker. Get out of here!"

With a flick of his cane, Sly commanded and the Devil obeyed. It struck Pudge with its metal claw, knocking him to the ground.

"Interesting company you keep, young Edison," smirked Sly. "The girl has some portion of brains, but this one..." He nodded to Pudge. "I can feel my intellect being sapped by his mere presence."

Eddie could feel his hands balling into fists. "Leave them alone."

"Oh, I have no intention of harming them. That is, unless you choose to be uncooperative." Sly pointed to the table where the belt lay, a few short adjustments from being finished. "Shall we finish what we started?"

Eddie stood firm. "Where's my father? What have you done with him?"

"He's around," said Sly.

"I'm not going near that belt unless you promise, *promise* to give him back to me."

Still groggy from being knocked to the ground, Pudge mumbled, “No!”

“And let me and my friends go,” Eddie added.

“Don’t do it, Eddie!” Roxie cried. “He lies. He’ll say anything to get you to help him.”

Eddie turned to her. “I know he does. But what choice do I have?”

“I’ll beat ‘em to a pulp as soon as I get up,” said Pudge, still curled up on the floor.

Sly raised his hand to his heart. “Complete your repairs, and I shall return your father to you. You have my word.”

With Roxie’s calls for him to stop ringing in his ears, Eddie turned back to the worktable. “I need a length of copper filament, a one-inch gear, some wax...” As he rattled off his list, Sly procured each item. The man stood by as Eddie worked, his face a mix of amazement and envy as Eddie’s hands flew over the invention.

When he was done, he lifted the belt and held it out to Sly. The man accepted it with hunger in his eyes. “At last...”

“I’ve done my part. Now, you do yours. Where’s my father?”

Sly’s eyes caught Eddie’s, and there was a dark twinkle in them. The kind of twinkle one got when they were about to deliver the punch line to a particularly nasty joke.

The man tapped the tip of his cane on the floor. "My friend, would you be so kind as to show this young man where his father is?"

The mechanical creature released Roxie and lumbered forward, gears whirring, metal wings rustling. It stood at attention before Eddie, towering over him. He could feel the heat coming off of its outer shell. Its blazing red eyes bore down into his.

There was a grinding sound, metal on metal, as a small hatch opened in the thing's stomach. More heat poured out of the thing like an oven. The creature reached inside, pulled something out and held it in its clawed hand.

The object it held was the shape of a brick. Black in color, its surface was covered in interlocking gears that spun and clicked.

"What's that?" Eddie asked.

"*That*, my dear Mr. Edison," Sly snickered, "is your father."

CHAPTER FOURTEEN

His father? Eddie stared at the object, not making a move.

"Go on. Take it, take it," prodded Sly, gleeful now. "Or rather... take *him*."

Eddie reached out to take the thing from the Jersey Devil. His hands were shaking so much he feared he'd drop it. It was warm, and he could feel the inner workings of the device buzzing and spinning inside.

"Don't worry, I'll save you the trouble of asking. This is one of my greatest inventions. I call it my Repository. I fashioned it before the great flood."

"What does it do?" Eddie asked.

Sly began circling Eddie, tapping his cane on the ground in a repetitive *tap-tap, tap-tap*. "It's really quite simple. Imagine everything you are – every moment, every thought, every memory you've got locked up safe in your brain. Now, further imagine that someone, such as myself, discovered a way to *unlock* your brain, allowing all of those little bits of you to filter down into another home. A mechanical home. A repository for everything that is you."

Eddie put two and two together. "You. You deposited yourself into this device."

Sly smiled. "Correct."

"That's how you survived the flood."

"Yes and no," said Sly. "While my mind remained safe inside that box, my body was washed away with the rest of the Mad Scientists of Voltaic Valley."

The whole scheme suddenly made sense. "My father..."

Sly turned to Roxie. "The boy seems to have pieced it together, don't you think?" Roxie spat in his direction and missed.

"My father must have found this thing. He was always picking up old junk."

"Junk?" Sly scowled, taking mock offence. "That's my magnum opus you hold in your hands!"

Eddie shifted. He stared back down at the black, metal brick. "And you tricked him. Somehow you tricked him into trading places. He got downloaded into this thing, and you got uploaded to his body."

"Downloaded? Uploaded?" Sly marveled. "I've been away far, far too long. There's *so much* to catch up on. But, yes. We swapped places, as it were."

"But... why?"

"Why?" Sly's anger boiled to the surface. "Because *he lived!*"

"Who?" Roxie asked.

Sly whirled on her, cane raised. Roxie cowered beneath his fury. "Thomas Alva Edison!" he raged. "Who else? I spent almost a century in mechanical hibernation, years alone in the darkness. My only comfort, the knowledge that *he* lay dead at the bottom of this lake. But when my Jersey Devil located my Repository, I awoke to find the name Edison *everywhere*."

"What are you going to use the belt for?" Eddie asked.

"What does it matter?" Sly laughed. "You have your father, I have the device. Our business is now complete. I'll have my mechanical friend show you the way out."

Pudge struggled to his feet. "We're at the bottom of the lake. I can't hold my breath long enough to get up top."

Sly snorted. "That's *your* problem."

Eddie dropped the Repository. It landed on the ground with a hollow *clunk*.

"What are you doing?" Sly snarled. "That's a delicate device!"

"I know, I know. It's your magnum opus," Eddie taunted. "But you know what? I think it's a hoax. I don't believe my father is inside that thing at all."

Sly fumed, furious at being challenged. "You don't believe me?" Sly screeched in his father's voice. "Go ahead! There's a button on the side. When pressed, he can hear you and you can hear him. Press it. Press it!"

Eddie picked it up. He turned the black brick around in his hands until he found the button. It was set in the side of the device below what appeared to be a small, mesh speaker. He pressed it.

"*...anything to try to get his way. Don't listen to him, Eddie. Please, don't listen.*" The voice that came from the speaker was rapid-fire and urgent, though it sounded nothing like his father. Instead, it was like one of those tinny, artificial voices that old, electronic toys made. Barely a human voice at all.

"You see," said Sly, obviously proud.

"Doesn't sound like him," Eddie scoffed.

"Of course it doesn't! The speech you're hearing is the product of a vibrating diaphragm. Oh, what's the point?" Sly pointed his cane at his metal creature. "Release them into the depths. Begin with Mr. Edison here. I grow weary of his company."

The Jersey Devil clamped a claw around Eddie's wrist and lifted him up off his feet. He winced as he felt his bones grind together, but he managed to hold tight to the black box with his free hand, if only barely.

Just as Sly turned away, a large beaker struck the ground next to him, exploding in a cloud of shattered glass. Sly turned in time to see Roxie picking up another beaker, preparing to throw it as well.

"What are you doing?" Eddie whispered to her.

"Buying you time to come up with a plan," Roxie whispered back. "So... come up with a plan, will you?"

Pudge tried to tip over a workbench, but it was bolted to the floor. Instead, he swept his arms across its surface, sending boxes of machine parts scattering across the floor. "Yo, Slime!" he shouted. "Clean up on aisle three."

As Sly started for Pudge, Roxie beaned him with a particularly heavy gear. Enraged, Sly swung his cane her way, and as he did so, a bolt of electricity shot out of the end. It struck Roxie square in the chest, causing her already wild hair to stand up straight. She was thrown out of her mismatched shoes as she absorbed the force of the jolt.

"You like to pick on girls, huh? Big man." Pudge shot Eddie a look that told him Pudge was about to do something amazingly stupid.

Which he did. He turned his back on Sly, dropped the back of his pants a few inches and mooned the evil genius.

Sly was flummoxed. "I'll teach you some respect," he sputtered.

He swung his cane in Pudge's direction. A second bolt of electricity caught Pudge in the rump, causing him to howl like an injured dog. He toppled over, every muscle in his body twitching violently with the burst.

"Enough of this foolishness," Sly said. "It's time I took my leave." He grabbed the belt and cinched it about his waist.

"Wait!" Eddie shouted at Sly. "Before you go, there's something I need to know."

Curious, Sly considered Eddie. The boy's companions were both out of commission. No harm in indulging the boy his final question. "And what might that be?"

"Come over here."

Sly grinned. "If you think I'll step within kicking distance you'll be sorely disappointed. Still, I'll come closer, if you wish." He walked until he was standing directly in front of Eddie, dangling in the grip of his mechanized servant.

Eddie stared at the man. He had so longed to see his father's face again, but to see it twisted by the malignant Sly nearly broke his heart. "You think you're pretty smart, don't you?"

Sly's eyebrows shot up, and he almost doubled over with laughter. "I've traveled over a hundred years into the future without the assistance of a time device, kept myself sane whilst trapped inside a mechanical box and reemerged not only with the means to return to my own time and bring the great Thomas Edison to justice but with a brand new body to boot. And you ask if I think I'm *pretty smart?*"

Sly made a short circle with his cane, and the mechanical monster gripped Eddie's wrist even harder. He felt it pop.

"Yes," Sly sneered. "I do believe I'm *pretty smart* indeed."

"Then why didn't you ask me about the upgrades I made to the belt that's around your waist?"

Sly's face dropped. He quickly glanced down at the device buckled about him. His hands flew to his waist to remove it, and as he did so, Eddie pursed his lips and whistled as loud as he could.

He felt his stomach drop as time came to a screeching halt. Not quite a halt, but near enough. And not for him, but for everyone *but* him.

Eddie could see Sly's hands moving ever so slowly toward the buckle. Thirty seconds. That's all he had. Aside from upgrading the belt's charge capacity, he had built in a thirty-second remote delay. Not a very practical upgrade – that is, unless someone who *wasn't* operating the belt might happen to want to give themselves a brief moment to take control of the situation.

Someone like Eddie, that is.

He glanced over at Roxie and Pudge. Both sprawled on the floor, victims of Sly's electric shocks. No time to worry about them right now. He had work to do, and the clock was ticking.

Eddie hooked one leg behind the Jersey Devil's back, using it to draw him nearer to the thing. "This sure would be easier if I had two hands and wasn't dangling three feet off the floor," he thought.

Twenty seconds. Not enough time! "*Don't rush,*" a voice in his head said. "*One step at a time.*"

He set the black box back into the mechanical creature's open belly, then reached inside and began pulling out wires. *Step one: ground the box. Step two: create a static link. Step three...*

He was just completing his last connection when his stomach flipped again, and he felt the air, which had gone heavy and stale at the commencement of the thirty seconds, lighten considerably.

The sound of the time travel belt dropping to the floor made Eddie look back toward Sly.

"What upgrades?" growled Sly. Eddie didn't say a word.

The man wearing his father's body limped over to where Roxie lay in a shivering heap. He placed the tip of his cane directly over her forehead. "Tell me, or I shall scramble the girl's brain."

Roxie lifted her head ever so slightly. Eddie could see that all of her moxie had fled – Roxie was terrified.

Eddie twisted around until he could look the Jersey Devil straight in the eye. "You there?" he shouted.

The metal beast let loose with a piercing whistle. A whistle that slowly morphed into a scream, then a gasp.

"*I'm here,*" the creature said.

Two things happened at once. First, the claw that had held Eddie above the ground opened, dropping him to the floor. Second, the Jersey Devil reached out and grabbed hold of the belt.

"What are you doing? No!" cried Sly. He pointed his cane at the beast. Nothing happened. The monstrosity raised the belt above its head with both claws as if it would rip the thing apart. Eddie rose and stood in front the mechanized beast.

"Stop!" Sly shrieked. He stepped away from Roxie. "What do you want? Tell me, it's yours. You want your friends back on the surface? Fine." He twisted the top of his cane. A hum filled the room and then... *poof!* Roxie flickered out of view.

Sly pointed his cane at Pudge. "Hey, wait a minute," said Pudge, but before he could complete his thought, he too flickered out of sight.

"They're safe?" Eddie asked, his voice steely.

"Yes, I swear," said Sly.

"Up on the surface?"

"Yes, blast you!" Sly hissed. "Now, put the belt down."

Eddie glanced back at the Jersey Devil. "You heard the man, Dad."

"*You got it, Sport,*" the creature boomed.

Sly's face went white. "Sport?"

Eddie stepped aside as the hulking metal brute dashed the belt to the ground. It raised one of its silver hooves and brought it down with a *crunch*. Sparks flew as Eddie's father, his mind now housed inside the monster's head, stomped on the device over and over until there was nothing left but bits of metal, glass and shredded pieces of leather.

Eddie squared off with Sly. The man was quivering with rage. "I guess you're stuck here in the present with us," Eddie said, sounding braver than he actually felt.

Sly raised his cane. His father took a clanking step forward, ready to launch himself toward the man who had stolen his body.

"I suppose you're right, Mr. Edison. But don't you worry. If I could master the nuts and bolts of my own time, imagine what I can accomplish today. I'll rise again, stronger than ever. And when I do, you shall be the first person on whom I will call. Until then..."

Sly swung his cane toward one of the enormous windows that lined the wall of the lab. An electric bolt shot from the end, hitting the fortified glass. The window cracked, tendrils of splintering glass spreading out across its surface like a spider's web.

Eddie caught one last look at Sly, one last look before he disappeared in a flash of shimmering light. The expression on the man's face was one of seething hate.

Bill Edison wrapped his metal arms around his son as the window shattered, water rushing in. "*Hold on!*"

Before he knew what was happening, Eddie was flying upward *toward* the broken window. He squeezed his eyes shut tight and took the biggest breath he could.

They hit the incoming water with such force that Eddie must have lost consciousness momentarily. When he came to, he was lying on the beach, the Jersey Devil standing over him. He coughed up a gallon of lake water, but other than that he was okay.

"*Where'd you learn that little trick?*" his father asked. "*Shifting me from the Repository into this?*" He banged his new metal chest.

"From Abel. He may be confused about a lot of things, but he makes a lot of sense."

His father leaned down to face his son, his blazing red eyes dimming ever so slightly. "*I've missed you, Sport.*"

"I've missed you too, Dad," Eddie said, trying to keep from crying and failing miserably. "More than you know."

His father put his powerful, steel arms about him. "*Let's get you home.*"

EPILOGUE

It was the middle of the night when the Jersey Devil dropped Eddie off at his home.

"I won't be far off," his father had said. *"Take care of your mother, Sport. Let's not tell her anything until I'm out of this... this..."* He couldn't finish. Eddie heard the mechanical equivalent of a sob welling up within the creature's metal chest, and he gave his father one last hug.

Its wings beating like industrial fans, the metal beast lifted up into the night sky and disappeared just as the porch light came on. The front door opened, and there stood his mother, her robe pulled tight around her, a look of both anger and relief on her face.

Eddie got the scoop while sitting crouched down in his father's chair in the living room while his mother stalked back and forth. Shortly after Eddie had 'borrowed' Lance's car, the police had shown up at the house. When Martha had gone to Eddie's room to retrieve him, she was shocked to find Reggie perched on the bed spouting, *"I don't feel so good,"* over and over again in between *rej-jips.*

One phone call from Martha, and Eddie's mother had turned around, abandoning her meeting in the city to instead join the search for her son.

It was only Jimmy Ticks' insistence to police that Eddie was trying to save him from a pack of bullies when he took Lance's car that kept Eddie from facing more serious repercussions. As it was, he knew he would be on the Mustache Mafia's hit list. Oh, would he ever.

The next day, Roxie and Pudge had shown up at his door. From the stern welcome Eddie's mother gave them, they knew their friend was in hot water. They also knew he was safe, and Eddie was relieved to learn that they were as well.

The fallout of his adventure consisted of being grounded for a month, having to deposit his lawn mowing money into an account to partially reimburse Lance for his wheels and, since he hadn't had any time to come up with a science project for Mr. Hubbard's class, Eddie knew he'd be facing some serious repercussions.

So it was that Eddie found himself fidgeting in Mr. Hubbard's class that last day of school. After the de-wigging incident, the crusty old teacher had decided to abandon any hopes of fooling people into thinking he had hair and, instead, had gone to the barbershop on the boardwalk and let them shave his head. Eddie had already heard kids whisper *chrome dome* behind Mr. Hubbard's back.

Jimmy Ticks had swapped seats with the kid to Eddie's left so he could be closer to his new friend. Every time Eddie glanced over, he'd catch Jimmy staring at him, a grin on his face. Ah, well. Befriending Jimmy Ticks was a small price to pay.

An overeager girl was wrapping up her science presentation – the exciting effects of watering bean sprouts with energy drinks. Mr. Hubbard kept watching the clock.

Somehow, Roxie had managed to pull off her presentation without a hitch. She had probably already completed it before the Jersey Devil whisked her away from the bowling alley. Pudge didn't fare half as well. Pudge stumbled through a presentation everyone in the room could tell was a last-minute effort, but at least he had a project to present.

"Mr. Edison?" Hubbard asked. "Should I take it from your empty desk that you are unprepared for this, the most important part of your grade?"

Eddie didn't meet his glance.

Mr. Hubbard shook his head. "What a shame. Not only have you deprived your classmates of a presentation, you've just guaranteed yourself the next month in summer school." Eddie could hear Pudge give a sympathetic moan.

Presentations over, Hubbard made a final note in his grade book and slapped it shut. The class tensed, ready to make a break for the door. "Wait," Hubbard said, tapping his watch. "You're mine for one more minute. And with that time, I'd like to let you all know that you have been the most lackadaisical, uninspired class that I have ever had the misfortune to..."

The bell rang – forty-five seconds early. "Too bad, Hubbard," Eddie thought.

Kids rushed the door, knocking into each other to escape their fifth grade teacher and get down to the business of enjoying the summer break.

"Summer school students stay behind," Hubbard commanded. "I've got business to take care of with you." Eddie and the other few unfortunates who had had their summers robbed from them remained seated.

Jimmy Ticks rose and leaned over Eddie's desk. "Wanna go play ball or something later, friend?"

Eddie shook his head. "Can't. I'm grounded."

Jimmy shrugged. "Maybe I can come over to your house. I've got a new card game. *Friendly Wizards*. Could be fun."

Eddie tried to hide his grimace with a grin. "Sure, Jimmy." At that, Jimmy bounded away like a happy dog.

Pudge and Roxie walked up. "Tough break, Einstein," Pudge said. "Still, things could be worse, huh?"

"They sure could," Eddie said. "Thanks, by the way."

Roxie considered him a moment, her head tilted. "I know how *we* got away from Sly."

"Yeah," interrupted Pudge. "He zapped us outta there, or something. Gave me a headache."

"But what about you?" Roxie asked. "How'd you get free?"

"And where's that guy Sly now?" Pudge added.

Mr. Hubbard slapped his desk with a ruler. "Ms. Michael, Mr. Rizzotti? Unless you care to join Mr. Edison in summer school, I suggest you see yourselves out."

Roxie and Pudge complied. As Roxie exited the room, she turned back and said, "That's Michaels with an S, Mr. Cupboard." And she was gone.

Eddie knew he'd catch up with them later. But what did he plan on telling them? That Sly was still on the loose? That his father was now the Jersey Devil? How much would be enough, and how much would be too much? He wanted to protect his friends as best he could.

"I'll figure it out when the time comes," he told himself.

Mr. Hubbard sat on the edge of his desk, his newly-shaven head gleaming in the fluorescent lights. He looked out at the few students who remained. "As you know, I have headed up the summer school program since the dawn of time. But I've been promising Mrs. Hubbard a trip to Miami Beach for years, and it looks like she's not going to let me out of it any longer."

Eddie and the others let out a hopeful gasp.

"No, that does *not* mean you are relieved of your academic duties. It simply means that while you are here trying to catch up with the rest of your class, I will be lying in the sun with a coconut drink in my hand."

There was a knock at the door. "Ah! Here he is," said Mr. Hubbard. "Students, let me introduce your summer school teacher."

With that, Mesmer stepped into the room. Eddie's eyes almost fell out of his head. "Mr. Mesmer, is it?" Hubbard asked.

"That's right." Mesmer grinned.

Mr. Hubbard gathered up his briefcase and papers. "Then, I'll leave you to it. Best of luck, Mr. Mesmer." Hubbard threw Eddie one last nasty look. "You'll need it."

Eddie watched as Mesmer sat at Hubbard's desk. His clothes were as mismatched and rumpled as ever. He picked up one textbook, then another, regarding each as a child would his vegetables. He dropped them in the wastebasket.

He glanced up. "What are you still doing here? Summer school doesn't start until Monday morning. Off with you, off with you!" Eddie's fellow classmates wasted no time in bolting for the door.

It was just the two of them. Eddie and Mesmer. "How could you?" asked Eddie.

"Pardon?"

"You knew he'd be down there in the old lab, didn't you? Sly."

Mesmer shrugged. "I might have had my suspicions."

Eddie rose, walked over to the teacher's desk and leaned in toward Mesmer. "And did you know he had my father locked up in that device of his?"

"I might have suspected."

Eddie shook his head. "Then why didn't you help me? You sent me down there all alone to face him. You said you'd be there if I needed you. You promised!"

Mesmer stood up, grabbed two erasers from the tray beneath the blackboard and clapped them together. A cloud of chalk dust rose, making Mesmer cough.

"Excuse me, am I boring you?" Eddie asked, growing angry.

Mesmer just smiled. "You're here, aren't you? You're standing right in front of me. You seem to be in one piece. I'd say if you had *really* needed me, and I hadn't shown up, we wouldn't be having this conversation."

"But...!"

Mesmer put a chalky hand on Eddie's shoulder. "I can't always help you the way you want to be helped.

Don't ask me why, because I can't tell you. Only know that everything I do is in both of our best interests."

"Sly doesn't know who you are," Eddie said. "When he was pretending to be my father, he told me he couldn't figure you out. That's strange, isn't it?"

"Yes, yes it is," Mesmer said.

Eddie waited for him to say more, but he didn't. Eddie sighed. He was done trying to make sense of things.

Outside, off in the distance, a piercing whistle filled the air. It might have been a passing train, but Eddie didn't think so.

"My dad is still trapped inside Sly's monster," Eddie said. "Will I ever be able to get him out?"

Mesmer clapped his hands together. Chalk dust flew. "Sounds like a fun summer school project to me!"

Coming Soon!

The Defenders of Ong's Hat

Book Two in the Mad Scientists of New Jersey Series

About the Author

Chris Sorensen is a Mad Scientist who lives with his wife Deborah and their two mutts in the Garden State of New Jersey. In his spare time he writes stories about the odd and unusual. He has dabbled in audiobook narration (200 titles recorded to date), played around with screenwriting (has a number of scripts in various stages of development) and tried his hand at playwriting (the Thin Air Theatre Company & Butte Theater of Cripple Creek, Colorado have produced fourteen of his plays). He has attempted to create a time machine of his own but has yet to succeed in this endeavor.

Acknowledgments

Thanks to my remarkable, creative and determined wife Deborah Graybill for believing in me.

Thanks to Tonya Copley and her students at Cresson Elementary School in Colorado, Holly Sturgill and her reading group at Benjamin Franklin School in New Hampshire as well as Ethan, Logan and Johnny for being early readers.

Thanks to Doreen Mulryan (www.doreenmulryan.com) for bringing the cover art to life and to Sondra Wolfer, Kevin Agnew and Nick Sullivan for lending their eyes.

And a final thanks to my nephews Gentry, John and Noah for letting their crazy uncle try out his storytelling skills on them.

Made in the USA
Middletown, DE
16 January 2017